"One of the sub...
— *SFRevu*

"When it comes to vividly layered characters and detailed world building, Shinn is a master at her craft."
— *RT Book Reviews*

On *Alibi*:
I really enjoyed *Alibi*. We root for the characters, we care about them, and we believe their interactions. And the conclusion is quite satisfying."
— Rich Horton, *Strange at Ecbatan*

"[Her] characters are vivid, distinctive, real people, all of whom are unique and appealing. It's the characters that make this story sing."
— Rachel Neumeier, author of the Tuyo series

On *Whispering Wood*:
"Fantasy author Sharon Shinn is known for her brilliant world-building and the layered richness of her characterizations, and she's in top form in her new Elemental Blessings novel, *Whispering Wood*."
— Mary Jo Putney,
    author of The Rogues Redeemed series

On *The Shuddering City*:
"Vivid worldbuilding, captivating characters, and a fascinating mystery. Readers won't want to put this down."
— *Publishers Weekly*

"A rich world balanced on the edge of disaster, with evocative, engaging characters, each with a piece of a desperately vital mystery to unravel."
— Martha Wells, author of The Murderbot Diaries

SHIFTER AND SHADOW

Also by Sharon Shinn

Uncommon Echoes
Echo in Onyx
Echo in Emerald
Echo in Amethyst

The Samaria series
Archangel
Jovah's Angel
The Alleluia Files
Angelica
Angel-Seeker

The Twelve Houses series
Mystic and Rider
The Thirteenth House
Dark Moon Defender
Reader and Raelynx
Fortune and Fate

The Elemental Blessings series
Troubled Waters
Royal Airs
Jeweled Fire
Unquiet Land
Whispering Wood

The Shifting Circle series
The Shape of Desire
Still-Life with Shape-Shifter
The Turning Season

Young adult novels
The Safe-Keeper's Secret
The Truth-Teller's Tale
The Dream-Maker's Magic
General Winston's Daughter
Gateway

Standalones and Graphic Novels
Alibi
The Shuddering City
The Shape-Changer's Wife
Wrapt in Crystal
Heart of Gold
Summers at Castle Auburn
Jenna Starborn
Shattered Warrior

Collections
Quatrain
Shadows of the Past
Angels and Other Extraordinary Beings

SHIFTER AND SHADOW

SHARON SHINN

FAIRWOOD PRESS
Bonney Lake, WA

SHIFTER AND SHADOW
A Fairwood Press Book
September 2025
Copyright © 2025 Sharon Shinn
All Rights Reserved

No part of this book may be reproduced or transmitted in
any form or by any means, electronic or mechanical,
including photocopying, recording, or by any
information storage and retrieval system,
without permission in writing
from the publisher.

First Edition

Fairwood Press
21528 104th Street Court East
Bonney Lake, WA 98391
www.fairwoodpress.com

Cover art © Thea Magerand
Cover and book design by Patrick Swenson

NO AI TRAINING:
Without in any way limiting the author's [and publisher's]
exclusive rights under copyright, any use of this publication to "train"
generative artificial intelligence (AI) technologies to generate text is expressly
prohibited. The author reserves all rights to license uses of this work for
generative AI training and development of machine learning language models.

ISBN: 978-1-958880-36-4
First Fairwood Press Edition: September 2025

Printed in the United States of America

To Ginjer Buchanan, who made it possible for me to bring these characters into the world in the first place.

CHAPTER 1

Dorrin Isle didn't look like a place people came to die. The island was so small that most of the western half seemed to be covered by a single picturesque village that sprawled across the tumbled, rocky land right up to the edge of a narrow beach. Twenty or thirty fishing boats pointed their sails into the gathering sunset and bobbed above the gently rocking ocean that unrolled into infinite darkness. Look too long at that vista, Donnal thought, and you'd feel your soul unravel. He'd never had much affinity for the sea.

But the village itself had a more cheerful aspect. The gray stone houses and wooden cottages were scattered haphazardly across the uneven land, a few clustered here, another one solitary behind a white fence, two more framing a garden plot that rioted with roses. Candlelight flickered behind most windows, smoke coiled up from every chimney, and long lines of laundry tied the whole place together with swatches of festive color. It was easy to imagine that, behind every closed door, families of robust fisherfolk gathered around their kitchen tables to dine on salmon and greens, tossing the scraps to packs of rambunctious dogs.

Well. Not every house would be bursting with loud, healthy people happy to be home at the end of a productive day. Somewhere on this island were a couple dozen people moaning on their sickbeds, some of them so ill they prayed for death.

Donnal wondered if it would really be possible to save them.

He and Kirra had been traveling off and on for close to a month, mostly in hawk form, winging their way from Ghosenhall on a series of autumn breezes. They had paused for a week at a homestead on the continent, where Kirra had taken human shape but Donnal had not. She had wanted him to, he knew. She hadn't said so—in fact, she'd gone to some trouble to keep her eyes turned away, so he couldn't see her pain and longing. She'd kept her voice noncommittal whenever there was a reason to speak. She didn't ask him to change. It was clear she had decided she never had the right to petition him for anything again.

He would have done it if she'd asked. And she knew it. And that was why she stayed silent.

At times he thought he might never again resume his human body. Living this way was almost unendurable, but any other option seemed impossible.

As they touched down on the beach, Kirra danced on her spindly bird legs as if trying to remember a specific type of balance. Her dark, heavy wings lifted and settled; her sleekly feathered head tilted from side to side. Slowly, her body puffed up and reconfigured itself, first rounder, then thinner, then taller, then paler. She was a half-formed shadow, then a solid shape, a fair-skinned woman with finely cut features and a mass of long golden hair. The dress that she manufactured on the spot was of a close linen weave that a rich woman might wear when she wanted to appear both elegant and practical over a long journey.

She shook out her sleeves and smoothed down the wrinkled skirt, then patted the contents of a small leather bag attached to her waist. "Do I look respectable?" she murmured. "Do you think anyone will ask where the rest of my luggage is? I suppose I'll have to produce a whole wardrobe. Unless the simple people of Dorrin Isle are so blinded by my charm and beauty that they don't require me to be fancy as well."

She glanced at Donnal, clearly not expecting a reply. She didn't make any observations about his own appearance, but she didn't have to. Even he knew it didn't make sense for her to go strolling into the village with a hawk on her shoulder. He scratched once at the pebbly sand, then allowed his body to flow into a completely new shape. Thicker, heavier, loose-jointed, and powerful. A black dog with layered amber eyes. It was almost as familiar to him as the form he'd been born into.

"Well," Kirra said. "Let's go see if we can find anyone on Dorrin Isle who isn't afraid of mystics."

Less than an hour later, they were ensconced in a cozy parlor in one of the larger houses, meeting with a woman named Eileen who had identified herself as the chief magistrate of the island. It was, Donnal knew, an unofficial and catch-all title. She had probably risen to the position because she had a knack for solving problems and handling disputes, and somewhere along the way she'd been given the authority to collect taxes and perform wedding ceremonies. That was how it generally went in the small towns throughout the country of Gillengaria. In some of the larger cities, the magistrates were chosen by the local marlords, or perhaps even the king. But in the more rural areas, the job usually fell to someone who knew how to get along with people and didn't mind the work.

Eileen and Kirra were sipping tea and munching on light refreshments. Donnal lay by the fire, his muzzle on his forepaws and his eyes half-closed, but he was far more alert than his pose would suggest. Kirra had no idea if they'd be welcome here. This whole venture was a desperate gamble—but the payoff had seemed so great that Kirra had ignored the dangers.

Typical Kirra.

"So, serra," Eileen said formally, setting down her teacup. She was a large, plain-featured woman with work-roughened hands and intelligent eyes, and it was clear she was not intimidated by the presence of a marlord's daughter in her house. "What brings you here tonight? Do you have news from Malcolm Danalustrous?"

"I don't. I plan to meet my father in Ghosenhall in a few weeks, and my hope is that I will be the one bringing news—from here on Dorrin Isle."

Eileen lifted her heavy brows. "You'll have to explain."

"I know that this place has become a refuge for people suffering from red-horse fever."

Eileen's faced clouded over and she nodded. "It has.

There's nineteen of them here at the moment, though I'd guess more than a hundred have passed through here over the last year or so." She gestured at the window, indicating some building invisible in the darkness. "There's an old barracks on the north side of the island. Your grandfather built it one summer when he feared an attack from Arberharst, but it's mostly sat empty the past fifty years. A while back, your father requested that we turn it into a sanctuary for the dying, so we did."

"That was kind of you."

"Malcolm Danalustrous paid to have the barracks renovated into an infirmary. And he pays some of the townspeople to provide food and laundry services to the patients. It was a kindness on his part more than ours."

"And yet," said Kirra in a soft voice, "there were reasons to refuse. No one knows much about red-horse fever, and many people are afraid to be around anyone who has it."

Eileen grunted. "Fisherfolk tend not to fear much that doesn't come out of the sea. Once you've faced down a squall on a small boat in the middle of the ocean, there's not much else that can scare you."

"Most reports I've heard say that it's not contagious. No one knows why one person catches it and another one doesn't."

"The only people on Dorrin Isle with red-horse fever are the ones who had it when they got here. None of the townspeople have come down with it." Eileen shrugged. "And none of the people who have arrived with the fever have survived it."

The magistrate picked up her empty teacup as if she would refill it, then simply held it a moment as she gave Kirra sidelong look. "We've had other mystics out here, trying to heal them, but there was nothing they could do. Maybe you're here because you think you can save these folks. But no one can stop red-horse fever."

"I can," Kirra said. "I've already cured two people."

The teacup slipped from Eileen's hands and shattered on the floor. Donnal lifted his head, prepared to leap to Kirra's defense if the need arose, but Eileen appeared shocked, not violent. She was staring at Kirra. "I didn't think it was possible."

"It's possible—but it requires a particular kind of magic. And some people are terrified of magic."

Eileen leaned back in her chair and studied Kirra with a narrowed attention. "Most people in Danalustrous aren't afraid of mystics," she said slowly. "Why would you think Dorrin Isle is any different?"

Kirra didn't answer directly. "I have some ability as a healer, but what I really am is a shape-shifter. I can take the form of any wild creature—or the face of any man or woman. And I can transform objects simply through touch." She extended her hand, her own teacup nestled in the palm. While Eileen watched, Kirra changed the porcelain to wood, then copper, then glass.

Eileen's gaze was fixed on Kirra's face. "And can you change them back again?"

"Easily," Kirra replied, suiting the action to the word. "Or I can leave them that way forever."

"I don't know what that has to do with red-horse fever."

"Magic can't cure the disease—but there's an herbal medicine that can. The problem is, the potion will kill a human. It only works on dogs and horses."

Eileen stared at Kirra in utter silence. Donnal pushed himself up to his haunches—not offering a threat, not yet, but reminding Eileen that he was in the room. She didn't even spare him a glance.

"I thought that shape-shifters could only change themselves," Eileen finally said. "I didn't think they could change other people."

"I'm the only mystic I know of who's ever done it."

There was another long silence. "And you think—you can change these sick people to sick animals—and—give them this medicine—"

Kirra nodded. "I've just come from a homestead in Danalustrous where I healed a young boy named Davie. When I changed his body and fed him the concoction, he was well within a week."

"And the other person? You said there were two."

Now Kirra smiled. "Lyrie Rappengrass. The granddaughter of the marlady. Ariane Rappengrass was eager to let me practice my magic on someone so precious to her."

Eileen thought it over for a long time. "Even people who aren't afraid of mystics might be afraid of that kind of magic."

"I know. And I know that the stories that come out of Dorrin Isle could make people fear mystics even more than they already do. But if I could save nineteen lives—or ten—or even one—I have to think the risk is worth it."

Kirra leaned forward, her gaze intense. "Will you help me? Will you introduce me to the patients? Will you persuade them that there is no reason to fear my magic?"

The expression on Eileen's face said she wasn't entirely convinced of that fact herself. "Most of them will be afraid even so," she said. She drew a long breath. "But I'll do what I can. If it were me? My child? I would take the chance. I would always choose magic and life over fear and death."

Kirra's smile was blinding. It had a sorcery all its own, because it made Eileen straighten in her chair and respond with her first smile of the evening. Kirra held out her reconstituted cup, as daintily as if she was at a society luncheon, and asked sweetly, "Is there more tea? We need to figure out what to do next."

There was nothing approximating an inn within the confines of Dorrin Isle, but a small stone cottage had been set aside for the use of visiting mystics, and Eileen arranged to take them there once she had provided her guest with a simple meal. She headed toward her small kitchen and cast a doubtful look at Donnal.

"I suppose he'll be content with a bone or a piece of meat?" she asked. "Never had dogs of my own, so I don't know."

Kirra hesitated, and Donnal knew she was trying to decide how to identify him. Why bother to reveal him as human if he was never going to appear in that form while they remained on Dorrin Isle? He met her eyes directly, something he had not done for what seemed like months now, and she studied him for an unsmiling moment. They spent so much time in animal shape—and they knew each other so well—that they had always been able to communicate without words.

Until they stopped communicating at all.

"A piece of meat is fine for now," Kirra said. "He might require more human food in the future. He's a shape-shifter, too, though this is his preferred form."

Eileen gave him a sharp look, then appraised Kirra a little more closely. Clearly, she didn't think highly of unchaperoned young women traveling around the country accompanied by men of questionable abilities. "I suppose it's different for serramarra," she muttered.

Kirra answered only with an unreadable smile.

After the meal had been eaten, and over Kirra's half-hearted protests, Eileen roused a neighbor to help her gather supplies that would make the visitors as comfortable as possible overnight. The short trip from the magistrate's house to the cottage proved to be something of an adventure. Full dark had fallen and few other buildings lay along their route, so it was virtually impossible to see the hazards on their way. The path was well-trodden but uneven, ascending a gentle hill before making a precipitous decline. It was obvious that the local women knew the way so well they didn't worry about where to put their feet, and Donnal's night vision was superb in this shape, but Kirra stumbled a few times. He guessed she was cursing silently, but she made no complaint. She hadn't even requested a candle to light their way.

He was pretty sure she saw it as another form of penance. *The way is hard, but it's the best I deserve.*

She would not say that out loud, either.

The cottage was cramped and low-ceilinged, nothing but a pool of chilly darkness when they stepped inside. Eileen paused at a table just inside the door and quickly lit a brace of candles that had been left behind. By their wavering light, Donnal could see two threadbare chairs set before the fireplace, where three cords of wood made a welcome sight.

"Bedroom's in there," Eileen said, pointing toward a shaft of darkness that might be a doorway. She gave Donnal another dubious look. "Only one bed."

"We'll manage," Kirra replied.

"Cloris brought clean linens," Eileen added, as the neighbor woman brushed past them to drop off the pillows and quilts she had carried up the hill. Picking up one of the candles, Eileen stepped deep enough into the room to reveal a long heavy table shoved up against the far wall. It held a limited selection of crockery and one large, battered pan. She set down the bread and meat she'd carried from her house and gestured to Kirra to add her own burdens—a jug of water and a bag of dried fruit.

"Someone will be by in the morning with more provisions," Eileen said, "but this should get you through the night. You'll find a pump out back when you need more water."

The other woman emerged from the bedroom. "There are linens and towels in the armoire," she said. "And room for your own things—if you brought any?"

Obviously, Kirra didn't feel like explaining how easily she could create her own clothing. "I thought my fine gowns wouldn't be right for working with sick people," she said. "Maybe I can borrow some simpler dresses while I'm here."

Cloris eyed her. "You're about Angie's size, I suppose." She nodded.

Eileen's gaze was back on Donnal, but she didn't comment directly. "Should we make a fire before we go? Even in early autumn, it can be chilly in a stone house on the edge of the ocean."

"Thanks, but I can do it."

"I didn't think a serramarra would have any practical skills," Eileen said with a flash of humor.

"I'm different from most serramarra you might have known."

"The only other one I ever met was your sister Casserah." She inspected Kirra again. "You don't seem to be anything alike."

"We're half-sisters," Kirra explained. "We're quite close, but you're right. We're very different. Casserah will never willingly set foot outside the borders of Danalustrous, while I can barely tolerate standing still."

Eileen glanced around as if checking for anything that might have been left undone. "The infirmary's the big building just over the hill and down the path," she said. "Come over around noon and I'll have all the families gathered to hear your story. And after that—well, we'll see."

"Thank you."

The women filed toward the door. "It doesn't lock," Eileen warned as she stepped outside.

"We don't have anything to steal," Kirra said. She didn't add the most pertinent point. *We can defend ourselves more ruthlessly than anyone you've ever met.*

"In the morning, then."

As soon as the women were gone, Kirra built a fire. Once the tinder caught, she knelt on the hearth for another ten minutes, simply staring into the flames.

Donnal watched her from across the room, observing how the firelight played along her fine skin and delicate features, how it turned her wild curls to spooled gold. Hers was a face made for laughter, but she showed no sign of merriment now. She looked exhausted. She looked sad. She looked as if she expected to feel both exhausted and sad for the rest of her life.

He didn't know how to mend her broken heart, not when his own was just as broken. Kirra was grieving for the man she loved, the man she had renounced, the man she had left behind in Ghosenhall a few weeks ago.

And Donnal was grieving for the woman he loved, the woman he could not possibly renounce, the woman he could not possibly have. Romar might leave his wife someday, Donnal supposed, and Kirra's story could have a different ending. But nothing would ever change the fact that she was a serramarra and he was a peasant's son. He had always known the gulf between them was impassable. He had thought it didn't matter—or, if it mattered, it couldn't be changed. Not until she fell in love with Romar Brendyn had he realized how completely his heart belonged to Kirra.

His heart. His life. Everything.

A moment longer she sat by the fire, motionless except for the impression of movement created by the flickering flames. Then she stirred, shook her head, and stood up.

"I don't know why it feels so late—it's not even close to midnight," she said. "All I can think is how much I want to sleep."

She glanced directly at him, seeming to know exactly where he was even though he doubted she could see him clearly in the dim light. "I suppose I should check out this bed. If it's anything like these chairs, it will be sagging in the middle and maybe standing on three legs."

She disappeared into the other room and he heard her rummaging around, speaking softly to herself. A few moments later, she reemerged. She had transformed her travel dress to a soft flannel nightgown and her boots to thick woolen socks. She had a quilt in both hands and a pillow tucked under her arm.

"It's *freezing* back there," she announced. "I'm going to sleep by the fire."

Once she had arranged the bedding before the hearth, she dropped down with a sigh of contentment. "Not much harder than the ground where we slept last night," she murmured. "And *much* warmer. I can't keep my eyes open. Good night." She yawned, turned on her side to face the flames, and seemed to fall asleep almost immediately.

Donnal waited twenty minutes, but when she didn't stir, he padded over and dropped to the floor again, curling into a loose ball at her feet. A moment later, he felt Kirra stretch out her legs and rest her toes against the fur along his spine. It was the last thing he noticed before he began dreaming.

CHAPTER 2

DONNAL CAME AWAKE SWIFTLY AND SILENTLY when he heard noises outside the door. Quiet footfalls, a low-voiced exchange of words, and then the sound of footsteps retreating.

No doubt, these were villagers dropping off the promised provisions. He allowed himself to relax from his sudden alertness, but he could tell he wasn't going to fall back asleep. A sullen dawn had started to peer through the closed shutters, and the cottage had started to fill with a tired, dusty light. Time to get up.

He came to his feet then paused, watching Kirra's face. She lay on her side, as if she hadn't moved an inch during the night, but he had felt her shift and turn half a dozen times. He figured it wouldn't be long before she was awake.

Crossing to the door, he nosed it open without difficulty because it appeared to have no latch as well as no lock. His guess had been right. Two baskets had been set up right against the outer wall, one holding cheese, bread, and a few other foodstuffs, the other containing an assortment of folded clothes. On top were a pair of dark trousers and a loose woolen shirt, both sized for a man.

Donnal hesitated for a long moment. When was the last time he had been in human shape? As they were on the road to Rappengrass after the disastrous outing in Nocklyn? He and Kirra had spent the afternoon chasing each other through the woodlands as their fellow travelers dealt with a broken-down carriage. Donnal had been in this very shape, while Kirra had assumed the form of a golden retriever. They had splashed through small creeks frigid with spring runoff and scrambled down hillsides laddered with branches brought down by summer storms. They had rested, panting, in a patch of mud and rolled to their backs to catch the sun on their bellies. It had been a sweet and carefree hour that he had intended to remember for the rest of his life.

And when they had both flowed into their human bodies, he had kissed her for the first time ever and told her he was leaving.

He'd meant it, too. He'd shifted into hawk shape and taken wing, flying north for upwards of fifty miles. He'd planned to keep traveling, past Helven, past Ghosenhall, maybe all the way to Merrenstow. He would fly so far that he would outrun his memories, leave behind that image of Kirra's face, stricken and stunned but unsurprised. She had known she could not expect him to stay, not when she was in love with another man. But he could tell she was struck to the heart by his sudden departure.

I can't say goodbye, she had told him.

He had intended it to be a permanent separation, the end of one life, the beginning of a new one, never mind that it would be a fractured, shredded, pointless existence devoid of any pleasure or meaning. But he had only managed to stay away a single day. Every time he went airborne, his body betrayed him; he found himself headed southward no matter how determined he was to maintain his route. Even when he sought a headwind to push him toward the northern border, it would always peter out. He would suddenly find himself riding a wayward breeze that blew toward the warmer reaches of Rappengrass.

He would break his heart if he continued to follow her, continued to witness her radiant joy in the presence of Romar Brendyn. But he would die if he left her.

It was late at night when he met up with the caravan that had been making the circuit of Gillengaria for the past few weeks as the shy young Princess Amalie formally introduced herself to all the marlords of the realm. In addition to a veritable army of common soldiers, the princess had been accompanied by two King's Riders named Justin and Tayse and two other mystics named Cammon and Senneth. Despite the fact that these four had inexplicably become some of Donnal's closest friends, he had not rejoined them in his human shape. He didn't particularly want any of them to know he had returned, though he suspected Cammon had sensed his presence the minute he arrived. He didn't want to be with them, but he couldn't be anywhere else.

So he accompanied the travelers for the rest of their journey, all the while keeping to one of his animal incarnations. He circled above them in avian shape as they rode; when they paused for the night, he turned himself into a fox or a wolf and settled just outside their campfires. During the days they spent at Rappen Manor, he took the form of a tabby and prowled around the outbuildings, hunting for mice. One of the undercooks liked cats, and she fed him kitchen scraps as a reward.

Then it was on to Ghosenhall, where something had gone wrong. Donnal didn't know what it was precisely, only that Kirra had repudiated Romar Brendyn, then fled the royal city. He had watched her make goodbyes to Cammon and Justin before flinging herself aloft in her own sleek hawk shape.

He hadn't even bothered to think about it. He had just dropped from his higher altitude and settled beside her, riding the same currents, never more than a few feet away. They had turned west, so he supposed she was heading to Danalustrous, but it hardly mattered. He had always followed wherever Kirra led.

It was different now, of course. Too much lay between them, her heartache and his own. Both of them were suffering grievous wounds that the other could not heal. He had kept to his animal shape for all the days and nights of their journey, though Kirra took human form for the week she spent healing the boy named Davie.

He thought it was easier for both of them if they didn't try to talk, didn't attempt to stumble through explanations and apologies.

Surely both of them remembered what he had said to her right before he left, the last words he had spoken aloud, might ever speak aloud.

I love you.

Better to remain a hound forever than to try to add anything to that simple sentence.

But.

Donnal sniffed at the carefully folded shirt, which smelled of soap and wool. Donnal's shape-shifting abilities didn't extend beyond the boundaries of his own body and the clothes he was wearing. *He* would not be the one visiting the sickrooms, calling upon magic to transform the ill and the desperate. And Kirra might be so focused on that task that she wouldn't notice the suspicious glances and the angry muttering of residents who considered mystics to be abominations. She might not think to take care of herself while she was caring for other people. She might not recognize danger until it was too late.

Donnal dropped his head closer to the basket and closed his eyes. When he opened them a moment later, he was a man.

For a moment, it was hard to get his bearings. The world showed a different set of colors and his ability to smell seemed, briefly, to have completely vanished. When he rose to a standing position, he was unsteady at first, forgetting the precise way to pose on two legs instead of four. But it only took him a moment to regain his human senses and snap completely into this comfortable, familiar frame.

He'd abandoned his clothes somewhere along the journey, so he was grateful for the donated items. Hoping none of the neighbors were near enough to be shocked by his nakedness, he picked up the shirt and trousers and circled the cottage, looking for the promised pump. It took a few tries to get it primed and flowing, and the first gallon was thick with mud, but eventually the water was clear enough for him to risk a thorough cleansing. He combed his fingers through his dark hair to tame it and pressed the water out of his close beard. He probably looked unkempt enough to frighten small children. With any luck, there would be a comb and maybe some scissors in the bedroom dresser, and he could make himself more presentable.

The trousers were both too long and too loose, but he rolled up the hems and tightened the belt and looked no worse than the average fisherman, he thought. The shirt had also been sized for a larger man, but once he had laced up the front, it fit well enough. Kirra could make some adjustments if she thought he looked too disreputable. He checked the clothes basket again and was pleased to find that the neighbors' generosity had extended to socks and a pair of boots—also too big, but also passable once he tied the laces tight.

He glanced toward the window, but there was no sign of Kirra, so he headed off to investigate. Behind him lay the path they had walked in darkness last night, but ahead of him, if he remembered correctly, was the way that led to the barracks-turned-infirmary. He set off in that direction, following the gravelly path as it skidded down a slope then slipped through a gap that cut through another low hill. The countryside was half boulder and half a tough ground cover that looked like a cross between moss and ivy. The few trees he spotted were skinny and wind-whipped, their roots clutching at the ground with a grim determination. Randomly, in patches of sun and shade, wildflowers shook their rebellious heads in a ceaseless breeze.

He stepped through the slim pass and found himself gazing at a dramatic vista. The ground sloped downward again, a green-and-gray tumble ending abruptly at a pebbled beach. The ocean spread out just beyond the shoreline, vast and forbidding and endlessly variable. To the northeast, reassuringly close, he could make out the undulations of the Danalustrous coastline. A few small fishing boats were drawn up on the rough beach—not as many as could be found tied up on the other side of the island, so this was clearly a secondary harbor. A handful of huts and houses clustered together in the windbreak of the broken hillside, and Donnal spotted the defiant blaze of another stand of summer blossoms.

A hundred yards beyond them rose the first building of any size that Donnal had seen on the island. It was a long, two-story structure assembled from gray stone and mortar, plain and utilitarian, though a profusion of windows and a collection of chimneys kept it from looking entirely grim. The exterior was softened by an extensive garden bordering one long wall, tidy rows of corn and tomatoes and squash and a few stalks that Donnal couldn't identify.

Beyond the barracks were a few additional buildings. A barn and what might be a dairy house. A couple of chicken coops. Not far past the cleared grounds, the hills reared up again and blocked the view. He couldn't be sure if more houses could be found on the other side or if this was the limit of civilization on Dorrin Isle.

He wondered how quickly he would go mad if he were forced to live in such a small, restricted space. Almost without exception, mystics were rovers, wanderers, restless uncontainable souls. It was hard to remember a time in his life when he had spent more than six months in one place.

Well. When he was a child. Living in his mother's house, surrounded by siblings and cousins on a scrap of land, old enough to have mastered the magic in his veins but young enough to have no idea how it would completely remake his life.

And then one day, Kirra Danalustrous had showed up at his mother's door, inviting him—commanding him—to come to Danan Hall. Her father had heard that this peasant's son had a mystic's power, and the marlord wanted someone to be a companion to his shiftling daughter.

And Donnal's life completely rearranged itself and the world itself changed shape.

Since then, he had followed her to every corner and border of Gillengaria, from the king's court to the Lireth Mountains. He couldn't even guess where they might head next.

He didn't know how they could manage to keep traveling together.

He couldn't imagine trying one more time to leave her behind.

As soon as he caught the scent of baking bread, Donnal turned and headed back toward the guest cottage. When he was close enough, he could see Kirra standing just outside the doorway, glancing around uncertainly. She was dressed in one of the gifted gowns, though even from a distance he could tell she had made subtle alterations, because it fit her perfectly. She'd braided back her wild hair, so her face looked exposed and vulnerable. Her expression was one of indecision and worry.

Wondering where he was, perhaps. Or fretting over what to say when she met with the sick and dying.

Or missing Romar Brendyn.

He came toward her slowly, silently, skimming

across the ground with the stealth of a woodland animal because that was how he always moved, no matter what form he was in. He saw her glance in his direction and then away, back down the path toward Eileen's house.

Looking for him in a different shape. Or looking for a different man.

Only when he got closer, only when it was clear that he was headed directly toward her, did she swing around and give him a closer inspection. He was near enough to see the emotions that flitted across her face before she locked down her expression. Surprise. Relief. Pain. Hope. Despair.

Nothing.

She didn't speak until he was about five feet away. "You've been off exploring," she said. Just as if they had been holding casual conversations for the past few months. As if nothing had happened, nothing had changed.

He answered in kind. "I didn't go far. Just across the hill to the infirmary. I didn't see a soul."

"I wonder how many people live on the island."

"Not enough," he said with such conviction that she actually smiled.

"Yes, I already have the sense that the place will feel very small and confined if we have to stay here for any length of time."

"I thought it took a week for Davie to recover enough for you to change him from a puppy back to a boy. Do you think we'll need to stay here much longer than that?"

"It depends on how many patients are willing to submit to my ministrations." He thought she was making an effort to keep her voice light. "You weren't there when I attempted the first transformations. I wasn't sure I would be able to successfully change Lyrie Rappengrass, so I practiced on Justin first."

That made him smile. Justin and Kirra had a contentious, bickering relationship that only rarely yielded moments of harmony. "*Justin?* Allowed you to practice magic on him?"

"I know! I think he was just trying to prove how brave he is. Not afraid of anything."

"Did you have any difficulties?"

"No—but Cammon was helping me."

The other mystic had a strange power that none of them completely understood. He was a reader, able to sense other people's emotions, but he could also soothe those emotions and calm a disordered mind. "Helping you how?"

She fished in the pocket of her borrowed gown and pulled out a small figurine carved from a chunk of tiger's-eye stone. It was shaped like a lioness, and the two of them had found it one afternoon when they visited an abandoned shrine to the Wild Mother. The almost forgotten goddess was believed to watch over all the creatures of the world—and to share her power with the shiftlings who could take the form of any animal.

"He knew that I always carried this talisman with me. He took it in his hands and he, I don't know, he poured his own magic into it. And his power flowed from the charm into me. I could feel it. It was almost easy to change Justin. And then Lyrie. And change them back."

But of course, Cammon was now in Ghosenhall

with their other friends. "Can you manage the magic on your own?"

She nodded. "I can. I did it with Davie, but it took more energy. I might not be able to complete more than one or two transformations a day. And if all nineteen patients take me up on my offer—" She shrugged.

"We could be here for quite some time, changing them into animals and changing them back."

She squared her shoulders. "So let's hope they start lining up right away so we don't have to linger in Dorrin Isle for an impossibly long time."

He nodded. "Well, let's have some breakfast. And then we'll head over."

Maybe fifteen people were awaiting them in a large common room of the infirmary. It appeared to be both a gathering space and a dining hall, because there was a kitchen to one side and rows of long tables down the middle. Donnal supposed some of the caretakers were afraid to leave their charges alone for even a few minutes, so they hadn't come down to learn the surprising news that Eileen had promised to share. Those who were present undoubtedly would carry the tale back to those who couldn't attend.

Most of the listeners were women, and a depressing number of them couldn't have been more than thirty years old. Red-horse fever tended to strike children; these were, for the most part, young mothers, although there were a few older women who might be grandmothers who could more easily be spared from the household. From the quality of their clothing, Donnal guessed that most were working-class folk, but at least two might be lower-level nobility. These Thirteenth House women—second or third cousins to the wealthier marlords—had money and connections but no real power or influence.

Despite their differences in age and rank, they all had a similar look, worn down by grief and exhaustion. Donnal thought, *Everyone is equal in the end.*

"I trust you've all passed a quiet night," Eileen began. "We've got a visitor today who wants to tell you about something that might provide you some hope for your sick ones."

There was a stir and a murmur among the listeners. A sharpness came to those haggard faces; the slumped shoulders drew back, and the heads jerked up. Everyone was staring at Kirra.

"Some of you might recognize Kirra Danalustrous, marlord Malcolm's shiftling daughter," Eileen went on. She might have slightly emphasized the word *shiftling*, just enough to get people thinking about what it meant. "I'd recommend you listen to what she has to say."

Eileen sat down and Kirra stepped forward. Her braided hair and plain gown made her seem like a country girl just in from doing the milking. A calculated look, of course. *I am one of you. I care about what you care about. No need to fear my wild ideas.*

"I know that all of you have loved ones who are dying of red-horse fever," she said simply. "I have learned of a cure for it, but you might find it terrifying. I am here to offer it to you, anyway."

The listeners gasped and whispered; one woman

uttered a short cry and buried her face in her hands.

"What is it?" a red-haired man demanded. He was husky and powerfully built, though not particularly tall. A man used to punishing physical labor. Maybe not so accustomed to withstanding emotional damage. "Nothing could be as terrifying as seeing my Josie die."

Kirra turned her eyes to him. "I am a shape-shifter, but I can change other people as well as myself. I can turn your Josie into an animal and feed her a remedy that isn't safe for humans. And when she is well, I can turn her back into your little girl."

After a moment of stunned silence, the crowd erupted into exclamations and questions and cries of *Is that true?* Kirra waited patiently until the clamor died down and a few people came to their feet to ask urgent questions.

"What is this remedy? If it works, why can't I give it to my daughter?"

"It's made of herbs that are poisonous to humans. If you feed it to your daughter, it will kill her."

"Where will you get these herbs? Do they grow on the island?"

"I brought some with me. And I have written to my father the marlord, asking him to send me more. They should be here within a day." Donnal thought Kirra had deliberately brought Malcolm into the conversation as a form of reassurance, because she didn't often trade on her exalted heritage. Malcolm was widely revered among the ordinary folk of Danalustrous; surely anything he condoned would be safe.

"But to make her into a beast! A cow or a dirty skunk!"

"As far as I know, the remedy only works on horses and dogs." She allowed a humorous quirk to come to her mouth. "Of the two, it would seem less awkward for your loved ones to take the shape of a dog."

"But if something goes wrong—! What if you kill my boy?"

"I can't swear there is no risk. But the chances are very good that he will live instead of dying."

"What if you turn him to a dog but you can't turn him back?"

"I have already changed two children, and cured them of the fever, and changed them back. I can do it again as often as I have to."

"How long does it take?"

"About a week. And then they're well."

Another murmur went around the room. That was near enough to see to the end of. After months of illness and deterioration, a week seemed like no time at all. But a week was much too short if this experiment went wrong. Donnal could feel the mood swing back and forth as the listeners thought through the implications of the timetable. A sick child might linger for a month, even two—feverish, in pain, but alive. A child felled by rogue magic could be gone in seven swift days. Sooner, if the sorcery went awry at the very beginning.

A woman sitting at the front table said, "I want you to explain to me—" but she was interrupted by a man standing in the back. He had the hulking shape of a blacksmith or a laborer, though his face was gaunt and his shoulders had been stooped by grief.

"I don't trust mystics," he snarled. "Nobody knows what wicked things they do when nobody's looking."

A few of the listeners rustled in their seats, suddenly uneasy, remembering the stories their friends and neighbors had told. *A mystic burned down my grandmother's house. There's a mystic in Ghosenhall, whispering lies to the king. A mystic can come into your house and go into your mind and make you do things you would never do . . .*

"Mystics are evil," said an older woman, pushing herself to her feet. "You prey on us because we're sad and weak and poor—"

Kirra kept her voice calm. "I am preying on no one. I will not touch anyone who is afraid of my magic. All I am doing is offering you—"

"All you're doing is taking our children and turning them into *beasts!* Who knows why? So you can sacrifice them in the middle of the night, maybe!"

A few more people hastily stood up, unsettled and uncertain. It was hard to tell if violence might erupt, but desperate people tended to act more irrationally than most. Donnal had been leaning against a side wall, but now he straightened up and began drifting toward the front of the room. Kirra could take care of herself. She could melt into the shape of a lioness and slash her claws across the face of anyone who presented a threat—or she could become a bird and dart away before anyone could touch her. But people might think twice about assaulting her if the man standing next to her suddenly turned into a bear.

Eileen was no bear, but she surged to her feet and glared at the agitated group. "That's a fine way to talk to Malcolm Danalustrous's daughter, who's done nothing but come here and offer you a miracle," she exclaimed.

"Anyone who's afraid of mystics, you can leave right now. But anyone who's brave enough to try to save someone's life—well, you just stay here and find out what you should do next."

That calmed the crowd, and most people resumed their expressions of worry and weariness. The man in back stormed out, followed by two others. Everyone else lingered, torn between the familiar vertigo of terror and the exquisite dizziness of hope.

Josie's father stepped up to Kirra, so close he could almost place a hand on her shoulder. "When can you start doing this magic?"

"Today, if you like," Kirra said. "Now."

He nodded. "Then come on upstairs."

CHAPTER 3

A BUZZ OF ASTONISHMENT RAN THROUGH THE crowd at the man's words. An older woman blurted out, "Carter! Aren't you afraid?"

He gave her a glance of contempt. "Afraid of everything," he said. "Afraid of doing nothing. At least this way I give my girl a chance." He swept his gaze around the room. "Any of you who want, you come along and watch."

"If you're willing, you can bring her down here," Kirra suggested. "So everyone can see."

"All right, then," Carter said, turning and pushing his way past the onlookers. Through the large open archway that led toward the center of the building, Donnal saw him head for the stairs and charge up them two at a time.

Kirra pivoted toward Eileen, who was still on her feet. "I suppose we'll need my potion quicker than I thought," Kirra said. She held out the small leather bag she'd carried all the way to Dorrin Isle, filled with a handful of precious herbs. "Can you take about a quarter of the contents and mix them into half a cup of porridge or something like that? Thank you."

Eileen nodded at Cloris, and the two women moved off to the section of the room that had been designated as the kitchen. Soon they were pulling out canisters and rattling dishes together.

Everyone else just waited, hardly stirring from the places they had been occupying when Josie's father made his sudden decision. It was almost as if they were afraid to move, so uncertain about the precarious balance of the world that they didn't want to risk tilting it in one direction or another.

It seemed to take a long time for Carter to return with his daughter in his arms, trailed by a small sobbing woman who was probably his wife. Donnal guessed that he had needed those extra minutes to persuade her that the chance was worth taking—or, who knew, maybe he hadn't convinced her. Maybe he had just wrapped the girl in layers of blankets and extracted her from the room over his wife's weeping protests.

"What now?" he asked Kirra, cradling his daughter against his wide chest. "Where should I put her?"

Kirra stepped closer and pulled back the edges of the blanket. Josie's face was so pale that her skin looked translucent; it was almost possible to see the blood pulse under the skin. Her cheekbones were painfully prominent and her strawberry blonde hair had thinned almost to the point of baldness. She looked to be either unconscious or sleeping. Donnal thought she might be ten years old.

"Why don't you sit on the edge of the table and put her head in your lap?" Kirra suggested. "You can hold her hand if you like—stroke her hair. That will comfort her if she wakes up and is afraid."

"She hasn't been awake for three days," Carter said.

Taking a seat on the rim of the nearest table, he arranged his daughter so that her head rested against his thigh and his large hand completely engulfed both of hers. His wife loosed a broken sob and flung herself on top of her daughter, crying *My baby! My baby!*

With his free hand, Carter took a firm grip on her shoulder and pulled her away, managing to tuck her under his arm and hold her more or less immobile. "None of that, Nona," he said, gruffly but kindly. "Let's see what the mystic can do."

Donnal pushed a chair over and Kirra dropped into it, her eyes intent on Josie. She drew the blanket back even farther, exposing the child's thin neck and bony shoulders. Carefully, precisely, she placed her hands at the base of Josie's throat, spreading her fingers up toward the loose jaws.

"Hold very still," she whispered.

No one in the room so much as breathed.

Josie's pale face seemed to blanch, then darken, narrowing from an oval to a triangular shape. Her smooth skin roughened, developed a layered texture, then a silky sheen. No, not silk—fur, short and curly, the ivory color of old milk. The child's snub nose was a puppy's sharp muzzle. Her stretched-out human body had become a wiry, compact four-legged frame.

Nona whimpered; a few of the onlookers gasped and uttered inaudible prayers. Carter just gazed at his daughter for a moment in silence before returning his attention to Kirra.

"Where's that potion, then?" he said in a level voice.

On the words, Eileen was at his side with a bowl

in her hands. Donnal thought she started back at the impossible sight—a small white puppy where a girl was supposed to be—but she set the bowl down as casually as if she carried a basket of bread. Its contents looked to be a watery pudding in an unappetizing shade of brown.

"How to get the mixture down her throat, that's the next question," Eileen said.

Nona pulled herself free from her husband's restraining arm. "Smear a little on her nose so she has to lick it off," she said. "That's what we used to do for sick dogs on the farm."

She reached for the bowl, but Carter elbowed her hand away. "You said the medicine wasn't safe for humans," he said to Kirra. "Can we touch it?"

"Yes. Just don't eat it."

Nona shoved his arm aside and dipped her fingers into the concoction. Now that the transformation was complete, she seemed to have committed herself to the fates; all she could do now was press forward. She spread a dollop of pudding around Josie's nose, rubbing until the puppy jerked her head back with a weak, irritable motion. When the pink tongue flicked out to wipe away the offending mess, Nona quickly dabbed a little more into the open mouth.

"There you go. That's my girl," she crooned. Her fingers were already back in the bowl.

"How much can we give her?" Carter asked. "How often?"

"As much as she'll take, every two hours. If you can get her to finish off this whole portion, we'll mix up another batch."

"When will the drugs take hold?"

"She's pretty sick," Kirra admitted. "Sicker than Davie or Lyrie, so I don't know. Maybe in a day or two. Maybe even by tomorrow morning there will be some improvement."

"All right, then." He came to his feet, his daughter still in his arms, the blanket trailing all the way to the floor. "We'll just go upstairs and keep feeding her." He nodded at Kirra and headed toward the door, Nona behind him, carrying the bowl.

There was another profound silence as they disappeared up the stairs. Kirra remained seated, her arms resting on the table, seeming perfectly relaxed and at ease. But Donnal, standing behind her, could read the strain in her shoulders.

"Anyone else?" she asked. "You see how simple it was for Josie."

"Maybe simple to change her *one* way," a woman muttered. "But we've no proof you can change her the other way."

"Oh, don't be ridiculous," Eileen snapped. "You can all see that the serramarra has done exactly what she said she would. There's nothing to be afraid of! And so much to hope for!"

"All the same, I'll wait a day or two before letting my son be turned into a beast," another woman said. "We don't even know if this precious remedy will work. I want to see some proof before I try anything so foolish!"

After a general murmur of agreement, the remaining crowd began to break up. Five minutes later, the only ones left in the dining hall were Eileen, Cloris, Kirra, and Donnal.

Kirra slumped in her chair. "Well, that went better

than I thought it might," she said. "I wasn't sure anyone would be brave enough to try it on the first day."

"And there will be more tomorrow, or the next day," Eileen predicted. "Once that little girl opens her eyes and starts regaining her strength. You'll see. The others will come rushing to your door."

Kirra started to answer, but yawned instead. Donnal was at her side before she could speak. "That took a lot out of you," he said. "Maybe you should go back to the cottage and lie down."

She yawned again. "The cottage seems so far away."

Before he could offer to carry her back, Eileen bustled forward. "There's a spare room right off the kitchen. Just a bed and some blankets, but you could sleep there for a while."

"I'd be grateful," Kirra said. She allowed Donnal to help her to her feet, though she walked to the small room under her own power. With a sigh, she sank to the narrow mattress and closed her eyes. The last words she said were, "Don't go far." She seemed to fall asleep almost on the instant.

Eileen stood in the doorway, eyeing Kirra with a worried frown. "Will it be like that every time she changes someone?"

"Maybe. Probably."

"That will wear her out for certain."

"She wants to do it."

Now Eileen transferred her speculative gaze to Donnal's face. "Why, I wonder? If it will cost her so much."

Because the world is a terrible and terrifying place, and she wants to conjure a flash of brilliant light to set against the encroaching darkness. Because she feels like she has done great harm, and she wants to redress it with an act of great kindness. Because she thinks that by healing others, she can heal herself. "Because she's a good person," he said aloud. "Because she can."

She nodded and did not answer.

They stepped out of the room and he closed the door behind them. "How many people will take her up on the offer, do you think?" he asked.

"I don't know. Maybe a dozen? Depends on how well Josie does and whether or not they decide to trust the serramarra." She surveyed him again. When he'd walked in behind Kirra this morning, she'd studied him for a few minutes, trying to get a sense of what kind of man would be traveling around the country in the company of a high-born mystic. Then she'd nodded as if in recognition. She knew working folk when she saw them.

"You might talk to some of the other parents," she suggested. "Most of them have never been in the same room with a noble before. But they'd feel comfortable talking to a common man like you."

Well, he didn't have anything else to do. *Don't go far*, Kirra had said.

He'd tried that already, hadn't he?

"Sure," he said. "Want to take me around and introduce me?"

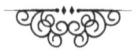

Eileen spent the next hour escorting Donnal down the second-story hallway, where all the patients' bedrooms were located. Sometimes the guests met them at the door, offered some curt version of *I saw today's demonstration and I'll be thinking it over*, and refused to allow them across the threshold. Other times, the parents welcomed them in, asked Donnal a dozen questions, and showed a mix of hope and indecision. But none of them asked to see Kirra. Not today.

Donnal was intrigued by the differences between all the individual rooms. They were all similar—small and overly crowded, crammed with beds for the patients, cots for their family members, a chair or two, maybe a table or a chest of drawers. But in some cases, the caregivers had made small, determined attempts to add personality with lacy curtains or vases of flowers or hand-knit blankets. They had tried to replicate beauty in a place where it did not naturally exist.

In one room, an entire wall had been turned into a colorful mural, a sunny woodland scene featuring dozens of real and imaginary beasts. Even as Eileen knocked at the open door, Donnal could see the artist still at work, kneeling in the farthest corner of the room with a brush in her hand. She appeared to be painting a pointy-faced creature just poking its head out from the base of a giant oak.

"Oh, I like that, he's got a sweet little face," Eileen said, stepping inside and up to the wall to take a closer look.

The kneeling woman rose to her feet and gave them a tired smile. She looked to be in her mid-thirties, short, dark-haired, and plump, though Donnal thought grief and worry had robbed her of some of her natural weight. "Lilah asked for a hedgehog and this was the best I could do," she said. Her voice was friendly and carried the broad accent of a country-bred woman. Not one of the few nobles here on Dorrin Isle. "I don't know that I've ever seen one outside of pictures."

Donnal crossed the room to inspect the image, smiling at her in return. He was a man who could pass weeks in perfect silence, not missing the need for speech, but in certain moods, at certain times, he could carry on an idle, relaxed conversation for hours. He was particularly at ease with the peasants and the working folk, the people of his own class. "I could model one for you, if you like," he said. "Let you draw one from life."

Now her face grew serious and she turned to study him, the paintbrush forgotten in her hand. "You were there with the mystic woman downstairs," she said. "Are you a shape-shifter, too?"

"I am."

"What do you think of her crazy plan?"

"I've seen it work. I think it's not so crazy after all."

"Something you might be willing to consider?" Eileen asked.

The woman hesitated. "If it saves Lilah's life? Oh, I'd do it. I would. But I don't know that *she'd* be willing, and I'd never force her. Even if means I'll lose her."

There was a rustling sound from across the room, and a girl's voice said, "Mama?"

All three of them turned that way to see a girl sitting up in bed, her dark hair mussed by the pillow, her round face creased with sleep or pain. She blinked rapidly at the sight of newcomers and pull the covers up to hide her bony shoulders. "Mama?" she said again.

Her mother hurried over, dropping the paintbrush on a cluttered table before bending over the bed. "Hello, love, did you have a nice rest?"

"I suppose," the girl said. She had only glanced at Eileen, whom she probably recognized; all her attention was fixed on Donnal. "I heard people talking."

"Yes, some very interesting visitors have come to the island today."

In the hallway, a voice called Eileen's name. "Someone needs me," she said, waving and walking out.

"Who are they? What do they want?" the girl asked.

Donnal stepped closer to the bed so she could get a better look, but not so close that he would seem threatening. "My name's Donnal," he said. "Who are you?"

"Lilah."

"And I'm Maria," her mother added.

"Would it be all right if I sat and talked for a while? I can tell you all about the reason I'm here."

Lilah considered for a moment, then nodded. Maria fussed about for a few moments, drawing up a chair for Donnal, pouring a glass of water for her daughter, then perching on the side of the bed. All this time, Donnal and Lilah regarded each other with interest. He liked the strong structure of her face, her inquisitive expression, her alert brown eyes. She looked like his youngest cousin, a fearless and irrepressible girl of fourteen. He guessed Lilah was close to the same age.

"I arrived on the island last night with the serramarra Kirra Danalustrous," he began. "Do you know who she is?"

Lilah's face sharpened with excitement. "Marlord Malcolm's oldest daughter," she breathed. "Is she as beautiful as everyone says?"

"Yes, and even more so," Maria said. "I couldn't believe the stories could really be true."

"More to the point, she's a shape-shifter," Donnal said.

Lilah frowned and sat back in bed so her spine touched the wall. "A mystic. Everyone says that, too."

"You're one of those who doesn't like mystics?" he asked casually.

Lilah waggled her head back and forth. "I don't know," she said. "It's just that people don't trust them."

"Some people," Maria put in. "Others are just fine with them." She looked at her daughter pointedly. "I am. I've never had a mystic do harm to me or anyone I love."

"Well, Tom and his father have seen more of the world than you have," Lilah said.

"That doesn't make them any wiser."

"Who's Tom?" Donnal asked, still casually.

Lilah might have blushed. Her voice was determinedly offhand. "Oh, he's just a boy who lives not far from our farm."

"Son of the richest man in fifty miles," Maria elaborated. "His father runs a shipping route out of Dormas. Has a lot of influence in our part of the country."

"And I take it he has a poor opinion of magic."

"Mystics have done a lot of harm to him," Lilah explained. "Sunk one of his boats! Right in the harbor! And killed off half his cattle one winter. And—" She bit her lip and looked at her mother.

"And lured his wife away one summer, or so the story goes," Maria added dryly. "Though I wouldn't think it would take magic to make someone want to leave that man. He's pompous and mean-spirited and thinks he's better than everyone else. Not even Thirteenth House, yet he wants everyone to treat him like royalty."

"And his son feels the same?"

"Oh, Tom's not a bad boy, or he wouldn't be if he had a decent father," Maria said, her eyes on Lilah. "I've seen him be kind once or twice when he didn't need to be."

"He's *wonderful*," Lilah gushed. "He'll talk to anyone, just like an equal, and he always gives coins to the beggar girls. *And* I was walking home in the rain once and he was driving by and he stopped and let me get in the wagon. And he gave me a blanket to cover my head! Though I was so wet by then it didn't matter."

Donnal exchanged a quick smile with Maria. "Ah," he said. "I can see why you like him so much."

"All the girls do," Maria said. She was choosing her next words with care, but Donnal could tell what she meant to say. "There's so much potential there for—certain kinds of trouble—but so far he's stayed out of it. He's eighteen, too, so he's already had plenty of time to make mischief."

"Points in his favor," Donnal agreed. "But he feels about mystics the way his father does?"

"You can't blame him," Lilah said. "Not after his mother."

"He wears a moonstone ring," Maria said. "Just like his father. The whole house is full of them."

Donnal nodded. Moonstones had been adopted as a holy symbol by the Daughters of the Pale Mother, the foremost religious group in Gillengaria. The Daughters reviled and persecuted mystics—even going so far as to round up and kill them, or so the rumors said. The touch of a moonstone could burn a mystic's skin, which the fanatics offered as proof that magic was malevolent. Donnal figured the opposite was true. The man who loaded himself up with moonstones as a way to harm someone else was the man who was cruel.

He kept his voice light and uncritical. "And you feel the same way?" he asked Lilah. "Like mystics should be feared and hated?"

She looked uncertain. "I don't know. I've never met one."

He smiled. "You've met *me*."

She instantly recoiled, and almost as quickly leaned forward, intrigued. "You're a mystic? Like the serramarra?"

"Just like her. Would you like to see me change shapes?"

She hesitated a long moment, studying him with her warm brown eyes, and then she nodded.

He chose an ordinary, unalarming animal—a shaggy black hound—and saw her eyes go round with astonishment. She didn't look afraid, though, so he made the short leap from the chair to the mattress, close enough for her to touch if she wanted. She lifted her hand, pulled it back, and then cautiously stroked the soft fur of his head.

"It feels *real!*" she exclaimed. "Just like my puppies back home."

"I think it is real," Maria said. "That's why it's magic."

Lilah was running his ears through her fingers. "Do you think he can understand us?"

"You'd have to ask him."

Donnal barked once in reply, startling Lilah so much she snatched her hand back and gazed at him a little fearfully. He opened his mouth in a slight canine pant and tilted his head to regard her. When she tentatively extended her hand again, he licked her fingers.

She laughed. So briefly it almost didn't happen, a glow of delight lit her sickly face. She looked like the child she was probably supposed to be. "You're silly," she said.

Donnal gathered his body tighter and flowed into the shape of a cat, a scruffy black-and-white tom who'd seen a few too many back-alley brangles. Lilah gasped but quickly recovered, reaching out again to smooth his rough fur. He felt her fingernails scratch gently down his back and arched his body in response.

"He looks like the cat the stablemaster keeps to catch rats," Maria observed.

"Do you think Donnal can catch rats, too?"

"When he's in this shape? I'd think so."

"That would be so *strange*."

Donnal squirmed out from under her palm and resettled himself on the bed, shrinking even more, shedding fur, shedding mass, adding feathers and a sharp pointed beak. Nothing as intimidating as a hawk, oh no—this was a summer songbird, black-winged and ruby-throated. He hopped onto her leg where it lay swathed under the covers and loosed a liquid trill of music.

"Do you think he can take *any* shape he wants?"

"I don't know. He promised me a hedgehog."

On the words, Donnal transformed, bulking up and blurring from bird to beast. He felt his thick coat of quills flow and ripple along his back. Lilah shrank away, but Maria leaned closer.

"Oh, I see. I haven't got the face pointy enough," she murmured. "And look at those little ears!"

"He *can* understand us," Lilah said.

"So it would seem. Do you have any creature you'd particularly like to see?"

Lilah had prudently refrained from attempting to pet this particular incarnation. "Something bigger," she said. "But not *scary*."

Donnal scrambled off the side the bed, making the leap without much grace in this rotund shape. As soon as his feet hit the floor, he began remolding them, making them harder, sharper, cleft in the front, tough enough to support the long muscular legs, the thick-barreled body, the long delicate face with its majestic crown of antlers. It wasn't a shape he took often, because too many hunters were eager to bring down a deer, whether for the meat or the trophy. When he needed speed, he tended to opt for a wolf or a lion. Fast *and* dangerous.

"Well, there's a fine buck," Maria said in an admiring voice.

Lilah started giggling. "It's so *funny* to see one inside a house!" she cried. "He looks so much bigger than the ones I see out in the wild."

Indeed, Donnal was carefully lifting and placing his hooves as he stepped back from the bed, trying not to scar the floor or knock anything over. Deer definitely weren't meant to be indoor animals.

Judging the demonstration to be more than sufficient, he bore down on his muscles again, rearranged his bones, and let himself readjust into the shape of a man. Lilah applauded and Maria smiled at him as he offered a small bow and dropped back into his chair.

"So that's what a shape-shifter can do," he said.

"That was marvelous!" Lilah said. "What does it feel like? It looks painful." She drew her knees up to her chest in an unconsciously self-protective pose. He guessed that her own small body was one unending ache.

"Doesn't hurt at all," he said. "Sometimes I feel a sense of pressure, or a kind of tickle on my skin. But it's no worse than stretching your arms over your head as high as they can go and feeling the way the bones in your back snap in place in a slightly different way."

"Can you take any shape you want?" Maria asked.

"The shape of any animal. I can't turn into a tree or a rock."

"Ugh. Who'd want to?" Lilah said.

"And you could understand us, couldn't you? It seemed like it."

He nodded. "Some of my senses change with each transformation. My eyes see more clearly, or my hearing is better. And I have a different set of instincts—a different sense of danger. But I'm still exactly myself. Everything the animal experiences becomes part of me. Its memories are my own."

Maria glanced at Lilah. "And the same thing is true for anyone who changes shapes? Anyone at all?"

He just nodded.

Maria turned and took both of her daughter's hands in hers. "Serra Kirra came and talked to us today about her shiftling magic. She says that there's a cure for red-horse fever, but the potion only works on animals. She says she can turn you into a dog, and feed you the potion, and make you well. Would you let her do that to you?"

Lilah was so shocked that she just stared at her

mother. Then she wrenched her hands away and buried them under the covers. "*Mama*," she exclaimed. "No! Why would you think—I can't give myself over to *magic!*"

Maria leaned closer, laying her palms over Lilah's knees, where they still made a tent out of the heavy bedclothes. "Why not? It would just be for a few days—"

"About a week," Donnal interjected.

"A week before you were cured, and then you'd be a little girl again."

"*Maybe* I would! Maybe I wouldn't! And then it would be all over me—wouldn't it?—for the rest of my life. People would look at me and see I was tainted."

"It wouldn't be like that," Maria said. She glanced at Donnal. "Would it?"

He shook his head. In truth, he had no idea. As far as he knew, the only two people who had ever been cured of the disease after being transformed by magic were Davie and Lyrie. He hadn't been around Lyrie at all, and he hadn't spent enough time with Davie to know if a glittering haze of sorcery trailed behind him, visible to anyone who was looking.

"Magic doesn't cling to you like mist. It doesn't mark you like a burn. It passes through you like breath. It just is, and then it's gone."

Lilah was shaking her head. "I don't believe you. You're just saying that."

"When you look at me, do you see magic?" he demanded. "Do I look different from any man you might see on the street?"

"No," she said reluctantly.

"Then what makes you think you will seem different? You could allow Kirra to transform you, and no one would ever know."

"Someone would know."

"How?"

"They'd ask how I was healed of red-horse fever! Which doesn't have a cure!"

He shrugged. "Tell them the diagnosis was wrong. It was some other disease, and you slowly recovered."

She was still shaking her head. *No no no.* "They wouldn't believe me. They'd find out the truth. And then no one would trust me. They'd point at me and they'd say, 'She's been corrupted by magic.'"

"Better corrupted by magic than dead in three months," Maria said sharply.

Lilah drew her legs closer to her chest, hunching down over her knees, making herself small and tightly defended. "Better to be dead than have people hate me," she whispered. "What would they say? Back home? If they knew? Some people would never speak to me again."

Maria threw her hands in the air. "Is this about Tom? That boy is never going to look twice at you! He'll be marrying some rich merchant's daughter, not a farmer's girl! Live your life for yourself, not for some fantasy in your head."

Lilah raised her head. "It's not about Tom! It's about everybody! And it's about *me*. I don't trust magic. *I'm* afraid of it. And it's *my body* that I'll have to live in the rest of my life."

Donnal nodded and rose to his feet. "So it is," he agreed. "You have every right to say no to something you hate and fear."

Her expression was suddenly woebegone as she gazed up at him. "Don't be angry at me," she pleaded. "I don't—I'm not afraid of *you*. I just don't—it's too scary."

He gave her a reassuring smile. "I'm not angry," he said. "But can I ask you a favor?"

She looked wary. "Yes?"

"Can I come back tomorrow? Or the next day? Can we talk about it some more? I promise you no one will make you do anything you don't want. Maybe after a while you'll find you're not scared at all."

She looked relieved, uncertain, and just a tiny bit excited. "All right," she said in what was clearly meant to be a nonchalant voice. "I won't change my mind. But I wouldn't mind if you came to see me again."

Donnal briefly met Maria's eyes, and she nodded. "Then I'll come back tomorrow."

CHAPTER 4

Leaving Lilah's room, Donnal made a quick pass down the second-floor corridor just to note how many families he hadn't met yet. Maybe five or six. He didn't like to intrude on them without Eileen at his side, so he headed back downstairs to check on Kirra. She was still sleeping, but she looked loose and comfortable, so he thought today's demonstration hadn't been too taxing.

"Should I be worried about her?" Eileen asked as he emerged. She was in the kitchen with Cloris and another woman, preparing an evening meal for the whole infirmary. Apparently when Malcolm Danalustrous outfitted a refuge, he was thorough.

Well, the marlord was thorough about everything. Donnal had never seen him unprepared or nonplussed or even surprised. Everything he could control, he did control; and when he couldn't control it, he kept himself mightily well-informed. A formidably intelligent and competent man, Malcolm Danalustrous. The only person Donnal respected more was the king himself.

"I think she'll be fine," he said. "But she'll be hungry

when she wakes up. If you could feed her, that would be a kindness."

"Of course."

"I made the rounds and counted only eighteen patients," he went on. "I thought you said there were nineteen?"

Eileen pointed. "There are a couple of women staying in the little house up the hill. The one with the blue shutters. They wanted more privacy than could be found here. One of them has the fever." She saw his expression and added, "I know. Usually it only strikes the young ones. But she has all the symptoms."

"Were they here when Kirra explained her plan?"

"I didn't see them. They keep mostly to themselves." Eileen's voice carried an undertone of disapproval.

Donnal tilted his head. "Something about them you don't like?"

Eileen made an unconvincing gesture of unconcern. "Two women traveling together like that—well, it's nothing to me! And they're Thirteenth House," she added. "At least, Geena is—the sick woman. I can't tell about her friend."

Donnal nodded. In Gillengaria, where the society was organized by class and station, anyone who existed outside the boundaries of a conventional life was always viewed as suspect. People might fear mystics, who could be powerful as well as different, but they were more likely to feel contempt for anyone who pursued an untraditional relationship.

From what Donnal had seen, mystics themselves had been ostracized so much that they didn't bother to hate anyone else who didn't conform to normal rules. Certainly, *he* didn't care if these low nobles were lovers. In fact, he hoped they were. How terrible to be completely alone when facing implacable death.

"Could you take me over and introduce me?"

She looked harassed. "I don't have time! But here." She picked up a loaf of fresh-baked bread, still in the pan. "Take this to Geena and tell her I'll bring eggs tomorrow. That'll give you an excuse to knock."

"Another kindness," he said, his face solemn but a smile in his voice.

She made a shooing motion. "I'm too busy to be kind."

He stepped outside and headed up the hill toward a solitary dwelling with a pitched roof, a weatherbeaten door, and a single set of blue shutters. An unkempt patch of grass out front was the closest thing it offered to a garden.

Halfway up the climb, he realized a woman was sitting outside on a wooden bench shoved up against the outer wall. The day was sunny, though the insistent breeze blowing in from the ocean kept the air relatively cool. Still, having spent only one night inside a house very similar to this one, Donnal thought he could understand why someone might take every opportunity to escape into the light.

As he got near enough, he could make out more details. The woman was wrapped in a much-patched quilt, having drawn it so closely around her body that only her head was visible. She'd leaned back so her shoulders were against the wall, and she'd lifted her face to catch the sunlight across her cheeks. Her eyes were closed. Her hair was either very blonde or going white, and she hadn't bothered to style it. The planes and angles of her face showed the refined features of a noblewoman. She looked to be in her early forties, though it was hard to be sure, and the red-horse fever might have aged her beyond her natural years.

He was pretty sure this was the sick woman. Geena.

Thinking she might be asleep, he approached quietly, wondering if he should just set the bread down and quickly retreat. But his overlarge boots scuffed against a patch of gravel, and she shook herself awake and sat up.

"Oh!" she said, startled but unalarmed to see a stranger on the scene. "Hello. How long have you been here?"

This close, he could clearly see the ravages caused by the disease. The fine skin looked chapped and raw; the green eyes were faded, the forehead creased in a permanent response to pain. Still, she attempted a friendly smile, and Donnal smiled back.

"On Dorrin Isle? Not quite a day," he said. "Here at your house? I just walked up." He held out his offering. "Eileen sent bread and promised to bring eggs tomorrow."

"Thank you so much. Bel will be pleased."

"Would you like some now?"

She shook her head. "I don't have much appetite. You can just set it in the house."

He placed the pan on a table he found right inside the door and allowed himself just one quick glance around the interior. Yes, very like the place he was sharing with Kirra, nothing more than a main room with a bare smattering of furniture, a low ceiling, and a sense of perpetual chill. Of her traveling companion, there was no sign.

He stepped back outside. "I'll go if you want to return to your napping, but if you're bored, I'll keep you company for a while."

"Oh, do stay," she said. She was leaning her head against the stone wall again, but her eyes were open and bright with interest. "I'm a social creature, and there have been so few people to talk to."

"I'm Donnal."

"Geena. How very nice to meet you." The crease in her forehead deepened with a slight frown. "There might be a chair inside."

Donnal sank to the ground at her feet. "I'm not fancy," he said.

She sighed, then smiled. "I *used* to be," she said. "Grew up in a fine manor. Married a man with an even finer house. Jewels and clothes and imported food and summer balls. That was my life."

"Until you got sick?" he guessed.

She gave a faint, exhausted laugh. "Oh, I was sick the whole time," she said softly. "Miserable in my marriage, with no way to put the feeling into words. Until one day I met Bel, and I thought, 'Oh! There are other ways to live!'" Not lifting her head, she slanted a look down at him. "I left him. Started traveling. I saw so many things I would never have thought possible. These past five years, I've been happier than I ever dreamed I could be."

"Good for you."

"You don't seem shocked."

"I've traveled a bit myself," he said. "I'm much happier on the road than staying in one place."

Her half-smile was appreciative. *So you're not going to comment on the fact that I left my husband for a woman.* "And what brought you to Dorrin Isle, of all places?"

"Same thing that brought you."

Now her eyes widened and she sat up straighter. "Oh no! You've developed red-horse fever? I'm so sorry."

"No. I've come with someone who's offering to heal it."

Her eyes narrowed and she studied him. "You arrived with the shiftling serramarra," she said. "Bel heard her talk this morning."

That was interesting, Donnal thought. Eileen had said she hadn't noticed Bel in the crowd. Maybe she'd hung back, not wanting to be seen, knowing that the others viewed her with disapproval. "So you know about the cure," he said. "Do you think you'll take it?"

She huffed out another sad little laugh and leaned back against the wall. "Oh, I don't think so."

"Is it that you're afraid of magic? I should warn you, I'm a shape-shifter myself."

"No, I've rather liked the mystics I've met! And the idea of being transformed into another creature is rather glorious. I am particularly enamored of the idea of turning into a horse."

"Then why would you hesitate?"

"I'm not sure my reasons would make sense to anyone else."

There was a note of finality in her voice, so Donnal didn't pry. "How long have you been sick?"

"Four months now? At first, I was just tired all the time. Then I was tired and feverish. And achy. Sometimes it felt as if all my bones had turned into knives and they were cutting up my body from the inside.

And then the nausea started." She grimaced. "It was two months before I was diagnosed and another month before I believed it. The physicians tell me that I may have three more months to live. Apparently the disease works more slowly in adults than in children, though I wouldn't call that a mercy."

"And how did you end up on Dorrin Isle?"

She seemed to phrase her answer with care. "When you have chosen an unconventional life, sometimes people are not eager to offer you aid. I needed a place where I could die in peace. Naturally, I could not return to my husband's house. My brother or my niece would have taken me in, but neither of them would allow Bel to cross the threshold, and that was unacceptable to me. Bel knew about Dorrin Isle, and here we are. And here we'll stay until—" She shrugged.

"It seems a comfortable place to live out your days."

"I suppose. We've only been here two weeks, and already I'm wishing I could be back on the road. Bel tries not to complain, but I can tell it's hard on her, staying in place like this. Thinking she'll be trapped here another three months. But she's promised she'll wait until the end."

Donnal thought about it. If Kirra were dying, he wouldn't leave her side, even if it took her a year to slip away, even if she lay there too weak to speak his name, too addled to remember it. And Kirra—that flighty, headstrong, headlong, rebellious, uncontainable spirit—she would maintain the deathwatch if he were the one who had fallen ill. It was strange to be so certain of something that he'd never even considered before. She might love another man, but she would never abandon Donnal to die alone. He supposed there was a comfort in that.

"Do you spend any time with the folks from the infirmary? Do the cooks bring you food, or do you make your own?"

"Bel doesn't like to cook, and I'm too tired. Mostly we fetch our meals from the kitchen. And I'm grateful for it, I am, but—I'm so tired of fish and chicken."

He smiled. "I thought I saw some vegetable gardens here and there."

"Yes. I should have said fish and chicken and tomatoes and greens and bread. But I miss—cakes and pies and good beef stew. And I miss apples. I find myself dreaming about them. It seems fruit doesn't grow on the island."

"The mainland's not that far away."

"No, and there's some boat trade between Dorrin Isle and the market towns on the coast. But no one thinks to bring back apples."

"Maybe you could put in a special request."

"Maybe I'll do that. Although, I don't even know. Can farmers grow apples around here?"

"They can. I take it you're not from Danalustrous?"

"Bel grew up here, but I'm from Kianlever. What about you?"

"Danalustrous born and bred."

"And friends with the marlord's daughter."

Friends. Maybe. It seemed like the wrong word, but the right word didn't exist. "Since I was a boy."

She eyed him a moment, and he thought she wanted to ask how such a friendship had come about. It was impossible to look at Donnal and think he was a member of the nobility, even on its lowest fringes. Just as it was impossible to look at Geena and miss the signs that she was Thirteenth House or better. But apparently she couldn't think of a polite way to word the question, so instead she asked, "What's she like?"

Before he could answer, a large orange tabby trotted around the corner of the house and made its way toward the bench. It came to an abrupt halt when it spotted Donnal and paused to give him a keen inspection.

"Looks like you have a visitor," he said.

Geena smiled and pulled the quilt down from her shoulders in a mute invitation. "There you are!" she exclaimed.

For a moment, the newcomer ignored her, all its attention focused on Donnal. Generally, animals liked him, but this one ruffled with a faint hostility. He sat completely motionless, and after a moment it lost interest in him. With a single fluid leap, it lifted itself onto the bench and stretched up to nuzzle Geena's cheek. Then it curled up against Geena's ribs and began to purr.

"You've made at least one friend on the island," Donnal said.

"She's good company," Geena replied. "But you were going to tell me about the serramarra."

As if he had the ability to put into words everything he knew and understood and believed and loved about Kirra Danalustrous. He searched for something suitable to say to a stranger. "She's something of a paradox," he said at last. "She has all the skills and graces of a marlord's daughter. She can dine with the king and discuss politics with any noble from here to Brassenthwaite. She's elegant and intelligent and loyal and charming."

"And yet?"

"She's a mystic. Which means she's unpredictable. Even Malcolm Danalustrous can't control her. She goes where she will and does what she wants. But that's any mystic for you."

Geena lifted a hand and began absently scratching the cat's head. "They say her father refused to disown her when it became obvious she had magic in her blood."

Donnal nodded. "Accepted her and made the whole world accept her. It's an extraordinary thing for a mystic to have someone as powerful as Malcolm Danalustrous on her side."

"Does he love her?"

Donnal smiled. "As much as he can love anybody. Mostly all he cares about is Danalustrous."

Geena leaned her head back against the wall. Her eyelids were beginning to droop, and he thought perhaps she had exhausted her store of energy for the day. "It seems as if she has had a very good life."

If you discount the fact that her heart is broken and may never mend again. Donnal came to his feet. "I think she would agree."

Geena seemed to force her eyes open. "You don't have to go."

"You look like you need to rest. But I'll be happy to come back tomorrow or the day after if you're up for company."

"Oh, I wish you would. This has been so delightful."

"I don't want to tire you out."

She gave him a sleepy smile. "Life tires you out."

Back at the infirmary, he found Kirra awake and consuming an enormous meal in the dining hall. A few other tables were occupied by residents gulping down hasty dinners, no doubt anxious about leaving their charges alone even for half an hour. Most of the others kept glancing over at Kirra, their faces showing complex emotions of doubt and hope. None of them approached her.

She waved him over, and as soon as he sat down, Cloris brought him a plate of chicken and greens. He couldn't help smiling, remembering Geena's complaint. "How are you feeling?" he asked Kirra as he took his first bite.

"Not as bad as I thought I might. But I'm not sure I could manage more than a couple of transformations in a single day without collapsing."

"Then perhaps it's just as well that our new friends still view you with suspicion. You can win them over one at a time."

She sighed. "I hope," she said, and took a long swallow of milk. "What have you done all day?"

"Set about making friends on your behalf. Visited as many patients as I could and tried to make mystics seem like good and kindly people."

"Any luck?"

"Not sure yet."

She picked up a biscuit and ate it in two bites. "Well, if anyone else does agree to the cure, we're ready for them. The supplies from my father arrived by boat this afternoon."

"Then all we need is a few brave souls."

Her face was sad. "Or people with nothing left to lose."

Cloris sidled back to their table in the diffident manner of someone about to sue for a favor. Kirra's expression didn't change, but Donnal could tell that she had picked up the same impression.

"Thank you, Cloris, that was delicious," she said with a practiced smile.

Cloris was twisting a dish towel between her hands. "I'm glad you think so. It's little enough we can do for the people who come here, so I try to put a good meal on the table."

"They're lucky to have you."

"I was thinking—I know you came here because of the red-horse fever, but I wondered—they say you're a healer—"

Kirra's voice was gentle. "Is there someone else on the island who's sick?"

"It's my husband. He's had a cough for weeks now and it doesn't seem to be getting better. I thought—but I know you're doing so much already—"

Kirra was immediately on her feet. "I'm happy to do what I can for him."

"Do you need me?" Donnal asked.

"I don't think so."

"Then I'll go back to the cottage and put things in order. Probably ought to make it an early night."

Kirra and Cloris departed, and Donnal made his way back to the cabin. It was still an hour or two before dusk, so there was time to open the shutters and air out the rooms and wipe down the surfaces. He found four pitchers and filled them with water from the pump, then chopped another pile of firewood. All the human activities relied on muscles he hadn't used for months, but he found it pleasant to stretch and pull his body in the old remembered motions.

He brought in a few armloads of wood, piled them on the hearth, then built a fire, sitting back on his heels to watch the flames leap up and hunker down. The warmth would be welcome. He remembered how cold Kirra's toes had been last night when she buried them in his fur.

From outside, he caught the sound of footsteps approaching, women's voices engaged in quiet conversation. Cloris's words were indistinguishable, but Kirra's floated clearly through the window.

"I think he'll start feeling better tomorrow, but let me know if he doesn't." Another few words from Cloris, low and heartfelt, and then Kirra's laugh. "No, no, I owe you for the wonderful meal! And you could be feeding me for weeks, so I'll still be in your debt. I'll see you in the morning!"

The door swung open and Kirra's silhouette filled the frame. For the first time in days, her voice sounded genuinely happy. "How delightful to actually be able do some *good* in the world for a change!" she exclaimed. "A simple infection of the lungs, easy to root out. I almost feel a sense of triumph. Do you—*oh*."

She had caught sight of him, sitting by the fire, waiting for her. Shaped like the black dog he had been when they arrived.

"Oh," she said again. The effort she put into keeping her voice nonchalant almost undid him. He could not bear to be the source of her smallest disappointment.

He could not bear to be alone in her presence, human. He almost could not bear it as it was.

"What a very good job you have done of making the place habitable," she said admiringly. "We shall be very cozy here."

CHAPTER 5

ONCE AGAIN, DONNAL WAS THE FIRST ONE AWAKE in the morning. As she had the night before, Kirra had abandoned the bed and slept on a pallet on the floor, her feet against Donnal's back. She did not comment on the arrangement and he did not pull away.

But he made sure he was out the door before she opened her eyes. Or maybe she waited to open her eyes until he was out the door. At any rate, they had both left the cottage before they once again encountered each other in human shape.

"Back to the infirmary we go," she said. "I wonder what today will bring."

The first thing it brought them was a small knot of people clustered around one of the dining room tables. Kirra and Donnal exchanged quick looks, then hurried over to see what had commanded so much attention.

They found a small white dog lounging on a bright blue blanket, her nose resting on her front paws. She looked tired, as if she had spent the day running madly around the island, chasing bees and butterflies. But her dark eyes were alert, and her fuzzy tail stirred faintly in welcome as Kirra and Donnal approached.

"Is this Josie?" Kirra demanded. She held her hand out, and Josie first sniffed it, then ran her pink tongue across the palm. "Look how much better she is already!"

Carter and Nona were leaning against the table, their arms around each other, their faces filled with awe. "We did just like we were supposed to. We fed her more of the potion every couple of hours, and then we let her sleep," Nona said. "All night long, every two hours, until it was gone."

Carter took up the tale. "And each time, she would just close her eyes and fall back to sleep, and we said to each other, 'Well, it might be a few days. We just have to keep doing what we're doing.' And this morning when we woke up, she was—she was *better*. She barked at Nona and licked her face."

"And she was hungry," Nona added. "It's been days since she would eat anything without coaxing, but I gave her some meat and she ate it *all*."

"This is wonderful!" Kirra exclaimed. "But you have to keep administering the potion. She's still weak, and her body is still fighting off the disease."

Nona broke away from her husband and practically flung herself at Kirra, wrapping her in a convulsive hug. "But she's *better*," she repeated. "She's going to get well. I believe it. I believe you."

"I'm so glad," Kirra said, holding the embrace for a long moment. Then she dropped her arms and turned to face the ten or twelve others gathered around the room, looking dazed and uncertain and excited. "Now. Who else is brave enough to try?"

At first, no one stepped forward. People shuffled their feet, looked at each other, looked away. One woman brought her hands up and covered her eyes as if she could not bear to gaze at the shape of hope.

"I am," she whispered. "Please help my Benjy. He's so sick. He's only ten years old."

"Take me to him," Kirra said. "I'll make him well."

This time, they didn't bother with theatrics in the main room where anyone could watch. Cloris paused in the kitchen to mix up the potion, while Kirra and Donnal followed Benjy's mother up the stairs. They were trailed by two other women who looked as though they were resisting with every step, but who were helpless to turn away from the sight of possible salvation.

Benjy's room was as cramped and utilitarian as the others, with piles of laundry and dirty dishes making it seem even smaller. His mother offered half-hearted apologies as she cleared debris off the single chair pulled up close to the bed, where a frail body lay in an almost motionless state. Benjy might have been small for his age—it was hard to tell—he was nothing but jutting bones and angular cheeks and tight skin brushed with the faintest sheen of sweat. His dark hair lay spread on the pillow like the shadow of approaching death.

"He's so sick," his mother said again. "Can you still help him?"

Kirra just nodded and sank to the chair, her hands already clasping the boy's. Behind him, Donnal could feel the press of the curious onlookers, and he stepped to the side so they didn't have to peer around him.

Kirra ignored everyone else, keeping her level gaze on Benjy's face.

Which smoothed out, roughened up, darkened, stretched. The thin shirt and trousers melted away as the child's body hunched up and reconfigured, transforming itself into the shape of a lean brown dog with curly fur. His mother tried to muffle a sob or a moan.

"Is the medicine ready?" Kirra said, not looking away from Benjy.

Cloris stepped forward to place the bowl in his mother's hands. "You heard what the serra told the others, Darcy," she said. "Feed him some of this every two hours until he's better."

Darcy took a deep breath. Donnal saw her hands clench so tightly on the bowl he thought it might shatter between her fingers. "Yes," she said. "I'll do that."

Kirra finally looked up, her eyes going straight to Darcy's face. She came to her feet and Darcy took her place in the chair. "I know you will," she said. "You'll be so strong for him."

One of the onlookers pushed past Cloris. "Me next," she said brusquely. "Come see my Will. Change him. Change him now."

Donnal watched Kirra closely as she performed the second transformation, worried about how much effort she was making. She swayed slightly as she came to her feet, and he was instantly at her side, putting his arm around her waist.

"What about you?" she asked a woman who had

followed her to the two sickrooms. "Are you ready?"

"I—I don't know. I—want to think about it."

Donnal was urging Kirra to the door. "Time for you to rest," he said.

Kirra kept her gaze on the other woman, turning her head to watch her even as Donnal pushed her from the room. "I can do it. I can do it now."

"You can do it later," he said, increasing the pressure in his arms. "Sleep now. At least for a little bit."

He was ready to pick her up and carry her if she didn't comply, but after a few more steps she stopped resisting, and he got her downstairs with no more protests. The little bedroom off the kitchen was already waiting for her, and she dropped onto the mattress with a heavy sigh. He thought she was instantly asleep.

"That's a sight that will never not seem strange," Cloris commented. "Turning a child into a beast."

"Think of the stories you'll have to tell your grandchildren," he said, stepping out of the bedroom and closing the door.

Cloris laughed. "I wonder if anyone will believe me." She headed toward the kitchen. "So what will you do while she sleeps?"

It wasn't even noon yet; it could be a long, dull day. "Visit the other patients," he said. "See who might be willing to be convinced."

Accordingly, he made the rounds a second time. News of Josie's miraculous improvement had flown around the barracks, and most of the other parents questioned him closely about what might happen next. They also knew about Benjy and Will, and he could see that the collective mood was shifting slowly from fear toward tentative acceptance. But there were some parents who still shook their heads, still radiated distrust and suspicion.

"Wait until Josie's a little girl again, and then we'll see," three of them said.

He honestly couldn't blame them. But he knew very well what they would see.

That Kirra was absolute undiluted magic.

It was just after noon when he stopped by Lilah's room to find Maria trying to coax her to eat. The girl was sitting up in bed, but slumping against the wall, her attitude listless, her face almost blank. But she stirred and straightened up when he stepped through the door, and a slight color washed over her cheeks.

"You're back," she said.

Maria threw him a grateful look. He imagined that Maria was grateful for anything that yanked Lilah, however briefly, from the stupor of illness.

"I am," he said, pulling up a second chair to sit by the bed. "Came to see how you're feeling today."

Lilah shrugged and pouted, turning her head away. Maria said softly, "She's eaten hardly anything. She's getting so weak."

"Well, now, that seems rude," Donnal said in his easiest voice. "All that trouble Cloris is going to, just to make sure you're fed! And you'll waste her effort?"

"I'm not hungry," Lilah replied. But she held her hands out for the plate her mother held, and she took a small bite of bread.

Maria watched her in satisfaction. "We heard the news this morning," she said. "Little Josie showed a marked improvement."

"She did. It's early, of course, but if she keeps getting better at this rate, she'll be well by the end of the week."

Maria shook her head. "I can hardly credit it."

"Two more will join her," Donnal said. "Boys named Benjy and Will. Do you know them?"

"We know everyone in the building," Maria said. She turned to appraise him. "Darcy really agreed to it? I would have put her last on the list."

"He's very sick. He didn't even open his eyes when we came in the room. I'm guessing Darcy realizes that Kirra is the only hope she has for him."

Lilah had taken a bite of cheese, which she hastily swallowed. "The serramarra," she said, showing some animation. "Tell me about her."

"What do you want to know?"

"What's she like? Is she clever? Is she kind?"

"She would have to be kind, don't you think?" Maria said. "To come to Dorrin Isle to try to heal these people—who are all afraid of her!"

It was almost impossible for Donnal to answer. *Kind* wasn't a word he was used to applying to any of his friends, who had all proved that they could be ruthless if circumstances required. Even Senneth, who would expend equal amounts of energy protecting the king or saving a poacher's son, could hardly be described as gentle. "She's generous," he said instead. "Thoughtful. Passionate. Willing to fight for something she cares about." He smiled. "Willing to play a part if she thinks that will get her what she wants. So many nobles are dazzled by her charm that they don't realize how intelligent she is."

"She sounds complicated," Maria said.

Liliah sighed. "She sounds wonderful. I hope I get to meet her."

"You will," said Donnal, "if you let her save you through magic."

Lilah flinched back. "I told you. I *can't*."

"But you said we could talk about it some more."

"Yes, but I said I wouldn't change my mind!"

"If this is about Tom—" Maria began.

"It's *not!* Well, it is, but that's only part of it. I'm just—it's too—" She drew her knees up to her chin and made herself the smallest possible shape. "It's *terrifying*."

Donnal nodded sympathetically. "I imagine so. Anything unfamiliar is."

"But you've done scary things before," Maria said in an encouraging voice. "Remember how you were so afraid to learn to swim? You wouldn't even put your head underwater. But now you can swim across the lake and back without even trying."

Lilah glared. "That was different. This is *bigger*."

"What would it take to make you stop being afraid?" Donnal asked.

Now she turned her frown on him. "I don't even know."

"Do you know what I was most afraid of? In my whole life?" Maria said. "I was afraid of having a baby."

That got Lilah's attention, and her gaze returned to her mother. "I didn't know that."

"My best friend died in childbirth. A year before I got married. And my mother almost died of it, having me. That's why my father left, because she never let him touch her again after I was born. I was certain I would die, too. I almost died of the terror before the labor pains even began."

Lilah's mouth was half open. "Then why did you even get pregnant?"

Maria's hand closed gently over Lilah's wrist. "Your father wanted a child so desperately. Just one, he said. And I loved him so much. I thought, 'Well, I'll have something of myself to leave behind with him when I'm gone.'"

"That was brave," Donnal said.

Maria's eyes were on Lilah's face. "And I've never regretted it, not one day," she said. "Having you in my life has been nothing but joy."

The words hung in the air, no one needing to say aloud the obvious implication. *And losing you will be total devastation.*

With a seeming effort, Lilah turned her gaze to Donnal. "What about you? What are you most afraid of in the world?"

He smiled and shook his head. "There's not much that frightens me, really."

"Heights?" Maria guessed. "Some people can't bear to stand on a mountaintop. They think they'll fall or someone will push them off."

He laughed. "I can turn myself into a bird and fly," he said. "And I'm not afraid of water, because I can become a fish and swim."

"So I suppose you're not worried about being eaten by bears or wolves, either," Maria said.

"Not at all."

Lilah made a sound of annoyance. "Having something *happen* to you isn't the same as being afraid to *do* something," she said.

"Oh, good point," Maria said. "What's something that would absolutely terrify you if you decided to try it?"

He stared at her and felt the room dissolve around him.

Nothing. Not a single thing. Except telling Kirra Danalustrous he loved her.

He had done it once, expecting to never have another chance, giving her no opportunity to recoil in horror or swoon with desire. Simply making the statement, not nerving himself to live with the consequences.

These last few weeks, they were both pretending he hadn't said it. Pretending it wasn't true. They had always pretended.

He would never be brave enough to say it again and then hope that she would answer him. The world would end before he could summon that kind of courage.

The world would end if he did.

He heard the slightest buzzing in his ears, and through it, the faint sound of Maria's laugh. "Oh, surely it can't be that hard to think of something scary," she said.

He forced himself to focus on her face, to bring himself back to this room and these people and the current conundrum. "I've never thought about that question before," he said. "Give me a few days and maybe I can answer it."

Lilah's voice was low and excited. "You do know," she said. "I could see it on your face."

"Lilah," her mother admonished.

"I could! He knows. He just doesn't want to tell us."

"Well, I don't think I would tell my secrets to nosy

young girls, either, if they were as rude as you."

"I'm not rude! And I told everyone *my* secret."

"Yours was hardly a secret."

Donnal shook his head and came to his feet, smiling down at her. "I like you," he said. "You remind me of my little cousin. Very tenacious. She always wears me down."

Lilah smiled back up at him. He could see that her strength was beginning to fade, and he knew that—for so many reasons—it was time for him to leave. "Maybe you'll tell me tomorrow."

"And maybe I won't."

"But you'll come back?"

He nodded. "Every day. I'll come back."

With Kirra still asleep, there was nothing on the island for Donnal to do, and he could feel the familiar restlessness prickling through his body. Only two nights sleeping in the same spot, and already he was itching to move on. Mystics weren't built to stay still, to have nothing to do but sit and think.

Or maybe he just couldn't bear the only thoughts that occupied his mind.

He headed down to the beach to see if the ceaseless agitation of the waves could satisfy his need for motion. Just for something to do, he shed his human shape, shrinking down, hollowing out his bones, trading his skin for the layered quills of feathers. He was a white gull, aloft in the air, feeling his wings catch and lift with the shifting breezes. Out to the west, the cloudless sky stretched forever over the limitless sea, which glittered and churned under a net of light.

He had told Lilah the truth—he wasn't afraid of the water—but it wasn't his natural element and he never liked to be far from land. He banked and pivoted toward the east, crossing Dorrin Isle at an angle and continuing on toward the reassuringly solid shape of Danalustrous. Once over land, he turned north and followed the coastline for a few miles, idly noting the inhospitable rocky coves as well as the gentler beaches and harbors. This stretch of the world was dotted with small fishing villages and the occasional larger town where trading vessels could dock with their assorted goods.

He'd been traveling about an hour when he came across one of those market towns and, on impulse, decided to stop. He scouted out a deserted stretch of shoreline before coming in for a landing. Even in Danalustrous, there were people who didn't care much for mystics. He made sure he was alone before shifting back to human shape.

He was a couple miles outside of town, but he enjoyed the hike once he made it to the main road. Wagons and carriages and horses passed him in both directions, but plenty of others were making the trek on foot, some of them pulling carts or carrying baskets and bundles. Most of them, he suspected, heading to the market stalls, hoping to sell or buy.

The town was only a few square blocks in size, but it proved to be a bustling and prosperous place. Shop owners kept their doors open to lure in customers, and every street corner featured some small farmer or craftsman selling goods from the back of a wagon.

When he came across a pub, he realized he was hungry, so he stopped for a quick meal and a glass of ale. The bitter liquid left a pleasant bubbling sensation against his tongue and brought an agreeable softening to his outlook.

You're feeling more human all the time, he thought. Maybe a good thing, maybe not.

Back on the streets again, he shopped with more purpose. It wasn't long before he came across a middle-aged woman selling bushels of fruit from an array of tables. Pears and apples, mostly, with a few baskets of blackberries off to the side. In bird shape, Donnal couldn't manage a whole bushel, so he negotiated for five pounds of apples, which the seller obligingly shoved into a small net bag.

"We're here every week, if you want to come back," she said. "No end of apples at this time of year!"

"I'll keep that in mind."

The transaction completed, he retraced his steps to the empty stretch of beach. For the return trip, he opted to take the shape of a golden eagle, with its marvelous wingspan and powerful talons. It was a bit of an effort to launch himself skyward with the bag in his clutches, but once he was aloft, it was a simple enough matter to ride the winds and coast his way back to Dorrin Isle.

He had lost track of time on his travels, so it was later than he'd realized as he descended from the heavens and circled once over the barracks. Smoke was rising from the kitchen chimney, and he could catch the scents of baking bread and grilling fish. Dinnertime already.

He made the short flight from the infirmary to the cottage up the hill, where neither of the occupants was in evidence. Dropping toward the ground, he transformed himself in midair and landed lightly on his feet. Not bothering to knock, he left the apples on the outside bench, then headed downhill toward the infirmary.

"There you are," Cloris said when he poked his head into the kitchen. "The serra was wondering. She's back at the cottage now. Are you hungry?"

"I could always eat," he said, and downed a bowl of soup without even bothering to sit. "How's your husband?"

"So much better! I can hardly get over it." She shook her head. "Everyone on the island's going to be coming to her with the smallest aches and pains. They'll never want her to leave."

"Hard to keep a mystic in place for a long time," he observed.

"That's what they say." She sighed, then brightened. "But at least she's here *now*. I guess we can't ask any more of her than that."

Donnal had spent his life, or so it seemed, not asking for any more than Kirra could give. "That's right," he said, setting down the bowl. "We can't."

Outside, he found that sunset was beginning to streak the western sky with flame and sorrow. He had only taken a few steps along the path before he was back in his accustomed dog shape.

Kirra was sitting outside the cottage on a chair that she must have dragged from the main room. "There you are," she said. "I suppose you were off having some kind of adventure while I was sleeping off the effects of magic."

He always felt safer approaching her in this guise,

so he came close enough to sit beside her and rest his nose on her thigh. She absently stroked his ears, keeping her gaze on the deepening blue of the sky.

"It was a good day, though," she said, as if he had asked for a report. Whenever he was in animal shape, she always shared her thoughts with him—or whatever thoughts she felt safe sharing, he supposed. "Josie seemed even stronger when I stopped by to visit after dinner. She's going to be up and running around by tomorrow. Will seemed very slightly better—already! I couldn't tell about Benjy, but at least he didn't seem worse. And one of the fathers came up to me when I was eating to tell me he was ready for me to change his son tomorrow."

She brooded a moment before going on in a low voice. "I wasn't sure anyone would agree to it, you know. I thought this whole trip might be waste of time, and I would just feel even *worse* about it. Wouldn't that be a terrible thing, to have this knowledge, this gift, and be unable to use it? I thought, 'Maybe I can save one of them. That's all I need. One life—one light to set against the darkness.' And now I think maybe there will be five. Or ten. A dozen candles in the night."

Even if he had been human, he wouldn't have had the right words to reassure her. *You are your own candle,* he would have said, except no one spoke such things aloud. *You are your own brightness. You are the only torch that lights the path ahead of me.*

Instead, he raised his head, making a soft whining sound deep in his throat, and lifted a paw to gently scratch at her leg.

"Yes?" she said, cupping his muzzle in one hand

and bending down to peer into his eyes. "Something you wanted to tell me?"

He scrambled up and licked her face, barked once, and licked her again. She laughed and bent down even farther, wrapping her arms around his neck. They stayed that way for a long time. Sunset had almost entirely fled before she finally let him go.

CHAPTER 6

THE NEXT TWO DAYS WERE MUCH THE SAME, except that Donnal stayed closer to the island during his afternoon forays. The daily expenditures of energy were wearing on Kirra just enough for the strain to start showing on her face, and he wanted to be within calling distance if she suddenly needed him.

She had agreed somewhat reluctantly to limit herself to two transformations a day, though they had briefly argued about it. "But if someone's *ready*," she said. "How can I say no? They might change their minds by the next day."

"How can you say yes if it means you exhaust yourself so much you can't help anyone else?" he countered. "You have to take care of yourself first."

She actually laughed. "I can't remember a time anyone has encouraged me to be *more* selfish," she said with a flash of her old insouciance.

"I doubt it will happen again."

The question didn't arise immediately, however, since she was only asked to change a single child each of those two days. Still, by the end of their fourth full day on the island, five children had been transformed into five dogs. Josie had improved so much that she was walking around under her own power, trotting up and down the hallways, sniffing at the kitchen counters, and sneaking out the front door if her parents weren't quick enough to stop her. Donnal could see that Nona was worried, but Carter wasn't—and in truth, it was impossible to miss the fact that Josie was on her way to complete recovery.

Of course, she was still a puppy. Of course, there was still one great test for both the mystic and her patient to pass.

The other four subjects were also noticeably better, though Benjy, who had been so close to death, was still too weak to leave his room. As Donnal roamed the halls most afternoons, he almost always found a few of the other parents lingering near the doorways of the changed children, sometimes holding low intense conversations with the other adults, sometimes merely standing outside, peering hungrily inside.

When Josie's a little girl again, Donnal thought. *Then they'll all be clamoring for a mystic's touch.*

He took every opportunity to greet them with casual friendliness, showing himself to be familiar, relaxed, unalarming. Most of them would have been intimidated by Kirra under any circumstances—these were not people who were used to conversing with a serramarra, particularly not one so incandescent as Kirra—but they were at ease with an ordinary peasant's son. Magic didn't seem so strange when it came from a man who looked like your neighbor's brother.

He spent an hour with Lilah every day, answering her endless questions. One of his chance remarks had made her realize that he had spent time at the royal court of Ghosenhall, and now she wanted to know every detail about the aging king, the mysterious young queen, and the reclusive princess.

"I just spent a few months traveling with Princess Amalie as she attended the summer balls at half of the Twelve Houses," he told her. "We had four mystics and four King's Riders in our entourage, and I can't even remember how many ordinary soldiers. You can imagine what a sight we made every time we swept up to some marlord's holding."

Maria looked over. "That's the first time the princess has been seen outside the royal palace since she was a baby, isn't it?"

He laughed at her. "Oho! So you're one of those who likes to hear all the gossip about the royal family?"

"Everybody does! But it's true, isn't it? Amalie has been confined to the palace for as long as anyone can remember."

He answered more soberly. "The king has been worried about her safety."

"But why?" Lilah demanded. "Do you think—do people want to *harm* her?"

He weighed his answer. There had been incidents both on the road and inside one of those luxurious mansions, but it was hard to know if Amalie had been the true target. He didn't know how far those stories had spread; he didn't know if he should be the one to repeat them.

Maria answered for him. "There have been troubles throughout Gillengaria," she said. "Some of the marlords scheming for the throne. Some of the Thirteenth

House lords scheming for their own lands. And mystics being run out of towns—stoned in the market squares—burned at the stake."

Lilah stared at Donnal with horror. "People want to *kill* you? Because you're a mystic?"

He took the risk of pushing her a little. "Why are you surprised? You've said yourself you're afraid of magic."

She recoiled. "Yes, but I—I wouldn't *hurt* someone. I just don't want anyone to hurt *me*."

"Some people think the only way to keep themselves safe is to get rid of the people they're afraid of."

"That's terrible!"

"People can be terrible," Maria said, her voice hard. She looked at Donnal. "Do you think there's going to be a war? My husband says it's almost certain."

"It's possible," he admitted. "The king is trying to prepare, in case it comes. But he's also trying to make sure it doesn't."

Maria shook her head and draped her arms around her shoulders. "Sometimes I think the world is an awful place."

Her eyes were on Lilah as she said it, and he knew what she was thinking. Even if war didn't come, even if the marlords didn't rise in rebellion and the fanatics stopped hunting mystics, even if the weather was fine and the crops were good and life mostly went on the way it was supposed to, the world would be bleak and bitter if Lilah died. A personal hell was always worse than a general tragedy.

"Sometimes it is," he said gently, coming to his feet and laying a hand briefly on her head. "But now and then, there's a scrap of hope that you can hold on to."

She nodded. She was still watching Lilah, who had sunk back onto her pillow and was already half asleep. "I'm trying," she said. "I'm still holding on."

It wasn't until the next day, their fifth on the island, that he had a chance to stop by Geena's cottage again. Kirra had performed two transformations this morning, dropping into an exhausted slumber immediately afterward. He sat by her bedside for about half an hour, but the day was so inviting that he couldn't bear to stay inside for long. He found himself outside and strolling through the infirmary's vegetable garden before it was even noon, and hiking up the hill a few minutes later.

He was pleased to see Geena sitting on the bench outside—as before, wrapped in a quilt and leaning against the wall as if she couldn't support the weight of her own head. When she spotted him, she straightened up and waved him over. Her face was lined with weariness, but her smile was full and genuine.

"I've been hoping you'd come by!" she said. "I wanted to thank you for the apples. Such a treat!"

He dropped to the ground before her, settling into a cross-legged pose. "Apples?" he repeated. "What apples?"

Her smile widened. "Oh, is that how you're going to play this? Very well, someone left me a bag of apples and I have been eating them every day and they have made me happier than anything I can remember for a hundred years."

"I thought you wanted to make a pie."

"Well, I did, but Bel doesn't cook and I'm too weak

to stand around chopping and baking, so we've had to improvise. Bel cuts them up and sprinkles them with spices and roasts them in the fire. *Very* tasty."

"I'll have to try that sometime."

"I suppose you flew over to the mainland to find them? But how in the world could you carry them back?"

He hid his surprise. Even people who didn't mind mystics tended to forget how varied and useful magic could be, how it could address problems that the ordinary human could not solve. But she seemed to have come to the correct conclusion instantly and without amazement.

"I took the shape of a golden eagle. It's not actually strong enough to carry off a baby, though people think it can, but it can certainly manage a bag of fruit."

She looked intrigued. "Is that your favorite shape?"

He shrugged. "I find it easy to take any form, and I'm comfortable in all of them. But I'm more likely to be a wolf if I'm in dangerous territory, or a dog if I'm not."

Her eyebrows lifted. "How often are you in dangerous territory?"

He thought over the past year or so as he and Kirra had made two long journeys across Gillengaria in company with Senneth and the King's Riders. There had been hazards at almost every stop.

"Lately, more often than I'd like," he said.

Before she could reply, the door to the cottage swung open and Geena turned that way. "Bel, come out, we have a visitor!" she called. "The mystic who brought me apples!"

Donnal's eyes were still on Geena, so he caught her swift and swiftly banished expression of surprise as the woman named Bel stepped outside. He politely came to his feet and turned her way. She was of medium height, somewhat plump, with unremarkable brown hair and a pleasant face. He thought she might be in her mid-fifties. She was dressed in loose trousers and a cotton shirt in a style similar to his own. Although she was smiling, she didn't exude Geena's natural warmth. In fact, he would have said she was trying to disguise a deep wariness behind a civil demeanor.

"Hello," she said. "We've been enjoying your gift very much."

That was something else that was interesting. Her appearance was that of a working-class woman, but her accent was refined enough to be noble. He tried not to show his sudden spike of curiosity, but merely offered a slight smile in return.

"I was glad to have a reason to make the trip to the mainland. There isn't much occupation for me here on the island."

Bel grimaced. "That is entirely true. Geena tells me I should take up cooking or sewing as long as I have time on my hands, but I've never been the domestic type."

"I *expected* you to take up whittling or carving," Geena retorted. "I think you'd enjoy having a knife in your hands so you could stab anyone who annoyed you."

"Oh, well, then there would be a trail of bodies across the island."

"Bel isn't exactly a docile and accommodating woman," Geena said. She seemed amused.

Bel sat beside her on the bench and gestured at her

own body. "As he could tell by my clothing. I hope he isn't shocked."

Donnal laughed as he resumed his seat on the ground. "I've been traveling around the kingdom with Senneth Brassenthwaite, who only wears a dress when she's forced to and is in every way the despair of her brothers, so no. I'm not shocked."

Geena leaned forward, her face sharp with interest. "I've heard such intriguing things about her! Is she really the most powerful mystic in Gillengaria?"

"I've never seen anyone who could match her."

"And her skill is fire?" Bel asked.

"Primarily. But she has other, smaller abilities. She can change her face a little. She is something of a healer, though it's a rough kind of sorcery. But mostly she can burn things down. Spectacularly."

"How did you come to know her?" Bel asked.

"Malcolm Danalustrous had brought me to Danan Court to be a companion to his shiftling daughter. And then he brought Senneth in to train Kirra in how to use her magic."

"That's astonishing," Geena said. "I knew Malcolm hadn't turned his daughter out of the house, but I didn't realize that he'd tried to make her stronger. I can't think of another marlord who would do such a thing."

"Well, Malcolm Danalustrous isn't like other men."

"Senneth Brassenthwaite's own father—he threw her out, didn't he?" Geena asked.

If he had ever doubted that Geena was Thirteenth House, her knowledge of and interest in the nobility put that doubt to rest. Gossiping about the marlords and their families was the favorite pastime of everyone in the Twelve Houses. "He did," Donnal said. "But she's mended relations with her brother Kiernan, who's the marlord now."

"Maybe that's what Malcolm was planning all along when he brought Senneth in," Geena suggested. "Making an alliance with Brassenthwaite. Aren't there a few younger brothers who might want to marry into Danalustrous?"

"There might be. But I don't think Malcolm is counting on Kirra to make a political marriage any time soon."

"Then what?" Bel asked. "Does she think to wed for love? That's not easy for a serramarra. Especially one who's a mystic."

For a moment, Donnal's chest was so tight that he couldn't draw breath. *Oh, she would marry for love if the man she loved was free*, he thought. *She would destroy her reputation, cut every family tie, abandon every friend, if she could be with the one man she can't have.*

"I don't know what Kirra plans in terms of marriage," he said, hoping his voice didn't sound choked and strange. "We don't discuss it."

"A woman doesn't have to marry to be happy," Geena said, glancing at Bel.

"She doesn't," Donnal agreed.

Geena sighed and leaned her head back against the wall, suddenly worn out. She added drowsily, "But I do hope the serramarra is happy."

Donnal came to his feet, very much ready for this conversation to be over. He said, "It's what I would hope for all of us."

Day six started out much as the others had, with Kirra and Donnal making their way to the infirmary to see which parents had mustered their courage overnight. The dining hall had drawn a larger crowd than usual, but it was easy to see why: A little white puppy was tearing around the room with a joyous energy, dashing up to onlookers, greeting them with a mock growl, and racing away, as if expecting them to chase after her. She bounded over to Kirra and tried to leap into her arms, barking madly. When Kirra laughed and sank to the floor, Josie frisked and yapped and ran her tongue across Kirra's face.

"She's ready to be turned back," Carter said. "Don't you think? She seems so healthy."

Kirra stood up, though Josie still romped at her feet. "Can you wait one more day?" she said. "Just to be sure? I have always allotted a week before, and I hesitate to take chances."

"We can wait a day," Nona said firmly. "A month. As long as it takes."

One of the other mothers pushed forward. "I can't wait any more," she said. "Now. Today. I've seen enough, and I believe you."

"So do I," said a second woman. "Come to my room next."

Donnal followed Kirra to the second floor, primarily so he could help her back downstairs half an hour later, when she was unsteady on her feet and trembling a little. Even so, he could tell she was pleased with herself—or something more than that. She was fiercely glad that she could so something tangible and real to alter the world's ratio of despair and jubilation.

"This has become so predictable that it's almost boring," he joked as they made it back to the dining room. "You perform a few magic tricks and then you sleep away the rest of the day."

"Yes, I have become quite dull here on Dorrin Isle," she said. "Whatever was I thinking to commit to such an unexciting schedule?"

Cloris and another woman were in the kitchen cooking, but Donnal's attention was immediately caught by someone nearer at hand. It was one of the few fathers who had taken up residence in the infirmary, a beefy young man with a ruddy complexion and a pugnacious manner. Gregor, that was his name. He had submitted to brief conversations with Donnal in the hallway, but never allowed Donnal into his room to check on the condition of his son. Donnal had put him down as one of the parents who would never allow his child to be transformed.

Now he was standing in the middle of the room, a look of anguish on his face and a small, still body in his arms. As soon as he saw Kirra, he stumbled forward.

"He won't wake up," he said desperately. "He cried out in the middle of the night—and then he got quiet—and he's hardly moving. He's still alive, I can feel him breathing, but he—can you fix him? Can you change him? I can't lose him, I can't—" He stuttered to a stop, breathing heavily, making no effort to hold back his tears.

Donnal tightened his grip on Kirra's arm, but she

shook him off and stepped forward. "Are you sure he's still alive?" she said gently, touching the boy's cheek and holding her fingers to his mouth to check for breath.

"He is," Gregor said. "I know he is."

"Kirra," Donnal said in a low voice. "You don't have the strength to manage another transformation."

She gave him a tired smile. "He doesn't have the strength to last another day." She gathered her energy and addressed Gregor. "Lay him on the table there. Yes, very gently. Now give me room."

She was too weary to stand, so she pulled up a chair and sat beside the sick child, gathering his listless hands in hers. "What's his name?"

"Emmet. After my father. He never could stand a mystic—my father, I mean—and what he'd think about this—but I can't not try. Not if I can save him."

Kirra nodded but kept her eyes on Emmet's face. Maybe it was Donnal's imagination, but it seemed that the transmogrification took longer than it should have, as if each individual bone had to be reshaped, each vein stretched and recalibrated, each patch of fur individually curled and colored. But a few minutes later, the boy was gone, and in his place was a thin hound with a short nose, a patchy reddish coat, and the look of an animal that was dying.

Kirra slumped forward in her chair, resting her head on the table so close to Emmet that his padded feet touched her unbound golden hair. Cloris, who had been watching from the kitchen, silently came over with a bowl in hand and showed Gregor how to smear the contents on Emmet's too-warm black nose. From the corner of his eye, Donnal saw the puppy extend the tip of his tongue to lick away the first drops.

He was more concerned with Kirra. "Can you stand?" he asked, putting his hands under her elbows. "Should I carry you to bed?"

"I'm fine," she said, not altogether convincingly, and managed to force herself to her feet. She wobbled a little but waved him away when he offered her his arm. "But I do need to lie down."

Behind him, Donnal heard Cloris giving Gregor encouraging instructions. "There, now, give him another dose, and another, just small bits, as many as he'll take."

The rest of her words were drowned out by a sudden sustained bellow of agony that rolled down from the second story and seemed to reverberate through the entire building. Cloris jerked around so quickly she almost dropped the bowl. Kirra staggered against Donnal as she turned to face the door. The roar came again, heartbroken and enraged, immediately followed by the sounds of lighter, questioning voices echoing up and down the halls.

"What's that?" Kirra whispered.

"Something terrible," Cloris whispered back.

But they all knew what it was.

The tormented cry came again, louder, accompanied by pounding footsteps and what sounded like a fist punching against doors and walls as someone charged along the upstairs corridor and down the stairwell. A minute later, a man burst into the dining room. His face was wild, his clothes were disordered, and his hands were beating at the senseless air.

"He's dead!" he sobbed. "My boy is dead! I thought—but you—and he *died!*"

It was the man who had spoken out so bitterly against mystics on their very first day at the barracks. Since then, he had refused to speak to either Kirra or Donnal, and Donnal had no idea how old his son was or what the child looked like. Donnal felt his heart crush down with compassion, even though part of him wanted to rage in return. *This is your fault! You could have saved him if you trusted us!*

Cloris set her bowl down and hurried over, trying to calm him with a hand on his arm. "Oh, Frank, I'm so sorry to hear it! Here, have a seat and I'll bring you some tea—"

"*I don't want tea!*" Frank roared. "*I want to kill the mystic!*"

And he flung himself across the room, his arms outstretched like broadswords slashing at Kirra's throat.

Donnal leapt in his path, already in wolf shape, his weight forcing both of them backward until they crashed to the floor. Frank cursed and writhed with a manic strength, sending Donnal tumbling away with a hard throw. Donnal scrambled to his feet and launched himself back at Frank's chest, knocking him down again before the man could do more than push himself upright. Frank continued to flail and punch, connecting with Donnal's jaw and his ribcage, trying to roll to his feet before Donnal brought him down again.

It wouldn't be a contest if Donnal could use his full strength; he could kill the man by clamping his jaws around the thick neck. But the Wild Mother knew he couldn't bear to murder a man simply for the sin of grief. All he could do was dodge the thrashing arms, dart in to nip Frank on the shoulder, on the chest, jump back to avoid a violent kick, spring forward again to bury his teeth in the corded muscle of the calf. Frank howled and Donnal tasted blood across his tongue.

Suddenly the room was filled with other figures, other voices, and Donnal backed off from the sobbing, panting man. It was time for human hands to intervene. Three men rushed over to smother Frank with their bodies, pinning him to the floor despite his continued struggles. He was still howling, but in a muted, hopeless way that was terrible to hear. One of the newcomers was Connor, and Donnal could hear him speaking soft phrases of commiseration. Donnal couldn't catch the exact words, but he knew they would do no good. He couldn't imagine anyone could say anything that would offer balm or comfort.

Still in wolf form, he twisted around to locate Kirra. She was on her feet, but swaying noticeably, her hand at her throat and her eyes fixed on the bereaved father. She didn't seem to be aware that she was crying. Nona was standing on one side of her, holding her up, trying to urge her to a chair, but Kirra wouldn't budge.

"Is he hurt? Will he be all right?" she demanded.

Connor looked at her over his shoulder. "Wouldn't say he's all right, not with a broken heart, but he's only bruised up." His gaze traveled to Donnal and stayed fixed there. "Didn't know the both of you were shapeshifters."

Cloris fired up immediately. "Well, *I* knew and *Eileen* knew," she said. "Wasn't a secret."

"Still. Didn't expect to see a wolf in the building," one of the other men replied.

"Frank tried to kill the serra. Went straight for her throat!" Cloris exclaimed. "Donnal did what he had to do to save her life."

Connor nodded slowly, holding the look another long moment before returning his attention to Frank. "Not sure what we're going to do about him," he said. "Might not be safe to just let him rove around."

The other kitchen worker headed toward the door. "I'll fetch Eileen," she said. "She can usually find a couple of island men to help out when someone's causing trouble."

Nona tugged more forcefully on Kirra's arm. "Come on. You're so weak you can hardly stand. You go lie down now."

Kirra was still resisting, so Donnal flowed into human shape. He was aware that everyone in the room was staring at him with an intense, somewhat fearful curiosity. They'd seen languid, lethargic children refashioned before their eyes, but this was something different. A powerful beast blurring into a wiry man so quickly their eyes couldn't follow the transformation. It was clear that, for the first time, they were realizing how dangerous he might be.

Nona dropped her hold as Donnal stepped over. He didn't bother to cajole, just swept Kirra into his arms and carried her into the side room. She murmured something against his shoulder, but he could feel her body already relaxing from its pose of stubborn protest. He laid her on the bed and shook the cover over her slumping body. Then he just stood there a moment, gazing down at her.

Cloris had followed him into the room. "Is there

anything I can do for her?"

"Sleep is all that will heal her. And then food once she wakes up."

"Will she be all right?"

He nodded. "It might be a day or two, but she'll recover. And maybe she'll be more careful in the future and not push herself too hard."

"I never saw anything like that," Cloris offered. "A man turning into a wolf. You were so *fast*. And the serramarra can do that too? Just become an animal any time she wants?"

"Yes, though she doesn't transform as instantly as I do. You can see the bones turning and the skin changing." He shook his head. "Normally, that's what she would have done when Frank came charging in. Turned herself into a lioness and fought him off herself. But she's used up too much magic today. She didn't have the strength to change."

"I thought Frank was going to *kill* her," Cloris said, shuddering. "Good thing you were right there to take care of her."

There will never be a day when I am not there to take care of her, he thought.

He had wondered, these past few weeks, if that could possibly be true. If he could spend the rest of his life trailing after Kirra, serving her when she needed him, fading back into the shadows when she didn't.

But it didn't even seem like a reasonable question anymore. The thought that Kirra could be wandering somewhere through the world, stalked by a danger that exceeded her strength, made his blood turn to boiling silver in his veins.

If he had not been in the room when Frank barreled in—

He turned toward the door. "I'm going to fetch a chair and sit with her a while," he said.

"All right," said Cloris. "I can't help her, but I'll bring you something to eat."

A few minutes later, he was settled next to the bed, sipping a mug of hot tea and balancing a plate on his knee. Kirra was deeply asleep, but it was a heavy, unnatural slumber, the kind he might expect from someone drained by a fever or battered almost to the point of death. He wished Cammon was here to repair her with his own fey magic, replenishing her strength, promising Donnal that there was no need to worry. He would be just as happy to see Senneth stride in, practically blowing everyone back with the sheer force of her personality. Senneth would lay her warm hands against Kirra's chilled heart and shove life and vitality back into her depleted body.

Red and silver hell, he would even be happy to have Justin on hand, sarcastic and scornful and always ready to fight. Justin would have knocked Frank to the floor with a single blow and taken on anyone else who thought it might be a good time to threaten a mystic. Justin couldn't do a thing to heal Kirra, but he would damn sure keep her safe.

Donnal leaned closer, wishing he could pour his own strength into Kirra just by force of will. Even as he had the thought, he remembered what she had said about Cammon managing just such a trick by holding Kirra's little lioness charm in his hand. Well, Donnal didn't have anything close to Cammon's power, but maybe love was as potent as magic.

He lifted the blanket and gently sorted through Kirra's pockets, finding the amulet in the second one he tried. It was smooth against his palm, very slightly warm from Kirra's body, a swirl of gold and brown and amber set with a single ruby eye. He curled his fingers as tightly as they would go, feeling the thin spikes of the stone feet dig into his skin. He placed his free hand against Kirra's cheek, so much paler than it should be, and bent low enough to rest his forehead against hers.

Wild Mother, watch her, he prayed. *Take anything you need from me and give it to her. Make her strong. Keep her safe. There is nothing else in the world I would ask of you.*

Maybe Kirra stirred slightly; he couldn't tell. Maybe there was a frisson of sensation in the hand that held the charm, in the hand that touched her skin. A tingle, a thread, a trickle of energy from his body to hers. Maybe her breath came more easily. It didn't matter. He just stayed there unmoving, guarding her sleep, listening for her heartbeat. Giving her whatever she would take from him. His life. Anything. Today and always.

CHAPTER 7

It was close to dinnertime when Kirra opened her eyes. Donnal had been weighing the relative restorative benefits of food and sleep, and he had almost determined that he should wake her up and feed her before allowing her to sleep again, so he was glad to be spared the decision.

"I'm so hungry I could die," she said in a voice that was almost a whisper.

He was on his feet. "I'll get a plate from the kitchen."

She didn't even bother to get up, just sat in the bed and finished off two entire meals. He was pleased to see that her hand stopped shaking after she'd eaten a huge bowl of stew and half a loaf of bread, and she gulped down most of a jug of water.

"Are you strong enough to go back to the cottage for the night, or do you just want to stay here?" he asked.

For an answer, she cautiously stood up, her fingertips resting on his arm for support.

"I'd like to go back," she said. "You might have to help me."

"Always."

They made their way slowly out the door and down

the uneven path, which had never seemed so twisty or rough. Kirra sighed with relief when they stepped across the threshold.

"I hope you were not planning on holding long philosophical conversations tonight because I'm just going back to sleep," she said.

"Bed or floor? Bed would be more comfortable."

"You wouldn't say that if you'd ever laid down on it," she retorted.

She did take a few minutes to clean herself up and change into nightclothes while Donnal pumped more water, built up the fire, and checked the supplies on the sideboard. Plenty of items there for her to snack on if she woke up ravenous in the night. Next time he flew to the mainland, though, he would bring back enough apples to add to their own rations.

When he came back inside with a final pitcher of water, she was lying on the pallet, facing the flames. But she turned her head when he walked in, lifting a hand toward him.

"Sit with me a while," she invited.

Unspoken was the rest of that sentence. *Sit with me a while, shaped as a man.*

He settled down crosslegged beside her, his back to fire. "I don't suppose you need me to tell you that that was a foolish thing to do," he said.

"Maybe, but it was the right thing."

"Maybe."

"And tomorrow will be spectacular," she said drowsily.

He was so consumed with concern for Kirra that he had forgotten other people existed in the world, battling their own fears and desires. "Tomorrow—you mean, when you change Josie back to a little girl?"

"That will convince the doubters, don't you think?"

"It will—if you're well enough to perform the trick," he said bluntly. "Don't even attempt it if you have the slightest doubt. A botched transformation will send *all* of the parents after you, not just Frank."

"I know," she said. "I might risk myself, but I'd never risk one of the children."

"But you're right," he said. "Once Josie is human again, I think most of the others will be clamoring for your magic. Promise me you won't try to do too much."

She didn't make the promise. "Most of the others?" she repeated. "Who might still refuse?"

"Three that I can think of. There's a three-year-old boy whose grandmother won't even let me see him. She's dripping with moonstones, so I don't think you'll be able to convince her that mystics aren't evil."

"That poor child."

"Then there's a teenager named Lilah." He considered. "Her mother is willing. Desperate, even. I think she'd let you change Lilah in her sleep if you'd do it. But Lilah keeps saying no."

She shook her head. "I can't change her if the girl won't agree. Do you know why she refuses?"

"I thought it was because of this young man she adores—he and his father despise mystics, and she doesn't want him to know she's been tainted by magic. But I think the truth is that she's terrified of the transformation." He leaned forward. "Maybe if you talked to her. She's a country girl and she's dazzled by the nobility. You might be able to charm her into agreeing."

"I *am* very charming," she agreed.

"And the third one—Geena—I haven't quite figured her out," he said. "She's a middle-aged woman, probably Thirteenth House. She's here with her lover, another woman who might be Thirteenth House, too. Geena is perfectly friendly, and she doesn't seem at all revolted by magic—she even said that she thought transformation would be glorious. But she won't undergo it."

"*Why?* If it would save her life?"

"She said her reasons wouldn't make sense to me." He shook his head. "I can't tell what her companion thinks. Bel. They both seem to have made their peace with the idea that she will die in the next few months."

Kirra's eyes were drifting shut. "Maybe I should talk to them, too."

"Change the others first," he said. "And then if you have any energy left, see who else you can save."

She didn't answer. She was already asleep.

For a few minutes, Donnal watched her face by firelight. He was pretty sure that all she needed was rest, but he couldn't shake off an insistent anxiety. He needed very little thought to decide to remain in human shape in case she needed him in the night.

Accordingly, he rose to his feet and moved briefly around the cottage, making sure everything was in order before settling beside her on the floor again. There was just enough room on the pallet for him to stretch out behind her, his stomach to her spine, his arm draped around her waist. So many nights, so many years, they had slept together this way, chaste as kittens, one or the other of them usually in an animal incarnation, both of them usually too tired to do more than murmur a goodnight.

Not always. Not always. Often enough, they had slept side by side in human shape—to stave off the cold of a winter camp or save the cost of an extra bed at an inn. Or simply to maintain the familiar routine they had followed so long they didn't even think about it.

It hadn't troubled Donnal for the longest time. He had never aspired to be anything more to Kirra than her servant, her shadow, her reflection. It wasn't that he didn't think of her as a woman; he didn't think of her as a woman he could *have*. Or maybe he just assumed she didn't think of him as a man.

Justin—Justin! of all people!—had scoffed at him more than once. "If you always show yourself as a dog, that's how she'll always see you." But it made no difference. Their roles were fixed, fated, forever, and that wouldn't alter no matter what guise Donnal wore.

He had always known she would marry some marlord's son and take her place in the glittering social circles of the Twelve Houses. He had always wondered if she would keep him with her in some role—relegating him to the servants' quarters, of course, but bringing him along as security when she traveled or trusting him with letters too delicate to send by any less devoted messenger. It seemed likely. He had tried to picture the life—a grand mansion, a settled existence, a reduced but respectable role—and assumed he would find a way to like it. Or at least endure it.

So he had not expected the burning, gaping well of loss and sadness that replaced his heart when she fell in love with Romar Brendyn. He was sure some people would call his reaction jealousy, but it felt bigger than that, and purer. It was a reordering of his existence. It was tantamount to the sun flaming out or the earth splitting in two, never to reknit its seams. It was a hollowing out of his body. Kirra was his core, and his core had been ripped away.

He hadn't had words for such an immense emotion. He hadn't known how to explain it either to Kirra or himself.

But of course, it was so simple.

I love you, he had said. It summed up everything and it changed nothing. He had kissed her, and then he had flown away.

And then he had returned.

Nothing was different, except that now he knew he couldn't be apart from her. He could live with that hot-coal sensation of grief always smoldering in his chest; he couldn't live not knowing, day to day, how Kirra went on in the world. The knowledge brought him a sense of peace even in the middle of the pain.

He didn't gather her more tightly against his body; he didn't tilt his head to bury his face in her tumbled hair. He just let himself sleep beside her, as he had so often slept beside her, and thanked the Wild Mother for the gift of this night.

She woke up once around midnight, jerking from her dreams with enough force to startle Donnal from his own. He could tell even before she spoke that she was uneasy and disoriented.

"Donnal?" she asked in an anxious voice.

"Here. Do you need something?"

Her hand found his and clutched it tightly. "No, I just—for a moment I didn't remember where I was."

"Dorrin Isle. Saving benighted children."

That made her laugh, as it was meant to. "Oh, yes, and we had *such* an interesting day yesterday!"

"How are you feeling? Any stronger?"

"I think so. But I'm hungry. In the middle of the night!"

He pulled away and stood up. "Just stay there. I'll get you some bread and cheese. Are you thirsty?"

"A little."

He fetched a plate of food, then renewed the fire while she ate every scrap in less than ten minutes. "There's more if you want," he said.

She shook her head, yawning and setting aside the plate. "No, I'm too tired. I'll talk to you in the morning."

She was still half-awake when he returned to the pallet and curled up behind her again. When he wrapped his arm around her waist, she caught his fingers in hers.

"This is nice," she whispered. "I've missed it."

He didn't answer. It was only another minute before she fell asleep.

Donnal woke with first light. Kirra was still sleeping, but she had started to toss and turn on the blanket, so he knew it wouldn't be long before she opened her eyes. He was on his feet and out the door before that could happen. He washed up at the pump and then headed for the barracks to see if anyone had started breakfast.

Cloris and another woman were in the kitchen, baking bread and mixing a bowl of eggs. "How's the serramarra this morning?" Cloris asked. "She was so exhausted yesterday."

"She wasn't awake when I left, but I think she'll be fine."

The other woman looked over. "This is the day, isn't it? Time to change Josie back?"

He nodded. "If Kirra is up to it. If not today, then tomorrow."

"People won't want to wait too long," Cloris said. "Until Josie is a little girl again—well, you saw how Frank acted—"

"I know. But we'll just have to see."

He loitered in the kitchen as long as he reasonably could, then carried a basket of food back to the cottage, taking the slowest route possible. But he needn't have worried. From behind the closed door, he could catch enough sounds to be certain that Kirra was already awake and dressed and moving around.

No chance of a quiet moment of intimacy, smiling before the fire, half-embraced after a long night curled in each other's arms.

He pushed open the door, letting the sunshine stream in behind him. "I brought breakfast," he said casually.

Her face, her tone, were just as casual. But he could read the strain in her mouth, something like disappointment tucked behind the guarded eyes. "Good," she said. "I'm starving."

A small crowd awaited them in the dining hall—a dozen parents, three cooks, a couple of islanders who had clearly been drawn by the promise of magic, and Eileen. Frank was nowhere in sight, so Donnal supposed he was still under watch in a cottage somewhere, unless one of the fishermen had ferried him back to the mainland. Gregor was there with Emmet in his lap, running his hand nervously over the red-brown fur on his son's head. The dog appeared to be sleeping, so Donnal couldn't gauge if he'd made any improvement overnight.

He glanced around. Yes, parents of *all* the changed children were present, drawn together in a tight knot, most with their arms crossed and their faces tense. But except for Emmet, none of the other children were here to witness the planned transformation. Donnal wondered if the caregivers had gathered in the hallway and whispered terrible suppositions to each other. *What if it doesn't work? What if Josie can't be turned back? What if she dies? I don't want my darling to see that.*

Kirra didn't seem intimidated by the walls of fear and worry that boxed in the entire room. She crossed the floor with a light step and smiled at the assembly. "It's good to see you all this morning," she said. "Where are Josie and her family?"

Someone stationed at the doorway called, "She's here!" They all waited in silence as footsteps pattered down the stairs.

Then a small white dog darted into the room and raced once around the perimeter, her feet scrabbling on the floor. Someone laughed at her infectious joy, and a few others murmured to each other. Donnal thought he heard someone say, "Well, that's a good sign."

Kirra dropped to her knees and held out her hands. "Come, Josie! Come to me!"

Josie danced up to her, barked in her face, and dashed away again. By this time, Carter and Nona had stepped into the dining hall. "You be good," Carter said to his daughter in a stern voice. "You go sit with the serramarra and do what she says."

Kirra kept her hands extended and Josie sidled up again, this time allowing Kirra to catch her shoulders, though she wriggled and tossed her head. Donnal sank to a crouch beside them.

"Should I hold her in place?"

"That might be a good idea."

As Donnal placed his palms on the delicate ribs, he could feel Josie's impatience, her inability to sit still. He could feel life and vigor and excitement thrumming through her veins and down her bones.

Kirra moved her hands to the long thin jawline and bent down to meet Josie's eyes. "Sit very quietly and look at me," she murmured. "Can you do that? Be very still."

Everyone in the room obeyed that command. None of the watchers shifted on their feet or cleared their throats or even drew a breath. The whole world waited.

Josie's narrow face grew round; the black nose faded to pink in a rosy face. Her body fluffed up, shed its hair, smoothed out, turned to flesh, turned to a torso and gangly limbs and a naked laughing girl. Nona shrieked and dropped to the floor, sobbing, gathering her daughter into her arms. "My baby, my baby," she moaned.

Everyone else was still frozen, still waiting, still needing that last piece of proof.

Then Josie threw her arms around Nona's neck. "Mama! Mama, can you hear me? Mama, I'm a girl again!"

And then everyone in the room was speaking and shouting and crying at once.

CHAPTER 8

THEY HAD TO CREATE A STRICT SCHEDULE BECAUSE suddenly everyone wanted the mystic's touch. Four of the parents who had held out this long begged Kirra to save their children, today, this minute, do it now. But of the patients who had already undergone metamorphosis, two were almost at the one-week mark, and their parents didn't want to wait a day longer than necessary to have their human children back in their arms.

Donnal could tell Kirra was willing to risk it—attempt three transformations a day until she had caught up with everyone who needed the initial alteration. He drew Eileen aside. "She'll do herself harm, and then she won't be able to help *anybody*," he warned.

Eileen nodded and bustled into the middle of the crowd that had gathered around Kirra. "No shoving, no nonsense, we're going to do this in an orderly fashion," she announced. Immune to wheedling and anger, she began parceling out the days.

Despite the grumbling of parents who would have to be more patient than they wanted, an air of euphoria hung over the group, filling the infirmary with a luminosity brighter than sunshine. People were jittery with hope. Donnal had never heard so much laughter from this small group, even as they trooped upstairs to their rooms and returned to fetch food or catch another glimpse of Josie.

Nona and Carter knew their role—to provide incontrovertible evidence of the glory of magic—so they stayed downstairs with their daughter throughout the long day. Josie herself was brimming with energy; her face glowed with health, her voice lilted with excitement. To look at her, no one ever would have suspected she had so recently been on the verge of death. She talked nonstop—to her parents, to the kitchen workers, to the other caregivers who gathered around to ask what the experience had been like, how much she remembered, how she had felt in animal shape, how she felt now.

"I remember everything," she said. "It was so much fun. And I feel wonderful!"

Kirra missed most of the activity. She had meekly accepted Eileen's directive to perform only one more transformation this day, and then she had stumbled to the little room off the kitchen to sleep the day away.

Donnal loitered in the dining hall to field questions from anyone who still had any, but by late afternoon, most people were back in their rooms, having come to their decisions one way or the other. He strolled down to the beach to feel the salt and the sun compete to paint their textures across his cheeks, then hiked slowly back up the hill, past the infirmary, and on to Geena's cottage.

She and Bel were sitting outside on the bench, and Geena waved as soon as she caught sight of him. "I hear you've had an exciting day!" she exclaimed as he dropped to the ground before them. "That little girl changed back from a puppy and completely cured! How astonishing and wonderful."

"Both of those things," he agreed.

"And none of the folks who saw this amazing sight started wailing about the sinful power of mystics?" Bel asked in a sardonic voice. "Calling for the serramarra to be stoned to death? Trying to kill her with their bare hands?"

Donnal assumed they had heard the story about Frank's attack. For two people who never mingled with the other residents, Bel and Geena always seemed remarkably well-informed. He shrugged. "Not today. Most of them are so desperate to save their children's lives that they have managed to push aside their horror and suspicion. For the moment, anyway."

"You don't seem particularly apprehensive," Geena remarked. "Have you never faced an angry crowd or someone who denounced you for your power?"

He thought about the Daughters of the Pale Mother and their threats of violence. He thought about a young woman who'd almost died giving birth to a mystic child because her father feared the magic in the baby's veins. Senneth had saved that child—and defied the Daughters, too.

"Kirra and I can change shapes quickly, which allows us to flee trouble if it ever occurs," he said. "Even so, if we're traveling alone or through small towns, we're careful not to flaunt our abilities. But if we're in the royal city, or visiting one of the noble Houses, we don't have much to be afraid of. No one would harm the daughter of Malcolm Danalustrous."

Bel's light laugh was hard to interpret. "Malcolm Danalustrous," she repeated. "There's a man who thinks he can reorder the world to suit himself."

It was an interesting thing to say. Generally speaking, the people of Danalustrous were fanatically loyal to the marlord, who was famous for his iron will, his even-handed justice, and his equally fanatical devotion to the land and the people who worked it. The people who spoke disparagingly about him tended to be those who actually knew him. Donnal covered his curiosity with a grin. "Most of the time, he's right."

"Do you like him?" Geena asked.

"He's not a man you actually *like*," Donnal said. He thought Bel snorted in amusement. "But I respect him greatly. He's powerful. He enjoys power. But I've never seen him misuse it."

"That seems like a high compliment."

Bel moved abruptly on the bench beside Geena. "I suppose there are good and bad marlords, just as there are good and bad farmers, and kind women and cruel ones." It was clear she had lost interest in the topic of the nobility.

Geena was resting her head against the wall, and now she turned it slightly to survey Bel. "You've been sitting with me so patiently all day," she said. "Why don't you take a walk? Donnal will visit with me for a while. And if I get so tired I need to lie down, he'll help me inside. Won't you?"

"Of course. And if you're too heavy for me to carry, I'll turn myself into a bear and scoop you up."

That made them both laugh, though Geena's expression was wistful. He guessed that she had always had a slender build, but the depredations of the disease had eaten away at her muscles and bones. He doubted she weighed much more than a hundred pounds.

Bel was already on her feet, though she tried not to seem too eager. "If you're sure."

"Of course. Go. You'll be much more cheerful if you can get away for a while."

"I'll be back in an hour. Or two."

She waved and set off, heading up the hill. Donnal and Geena watched in silence until she topped the rise and disappeared.

Then Geena sighed. "This is harder on her than it is on me."

"That seems difficult to believe."

"I'm content. Or at least resigned. Bel is—not."

"Because she's facing the prospect of a life without you?" When she didn't answer, he hitched himself forward, close enough now that he could have touched her knee. "It doesn't have to come to that. You heard the news. Kirra changed Josie—*saved* her. She can save you."

Geena was shaking her head, her expression adamant. "You don't understand. I'm not afraid of dying. I'm afraid of living."

He stared at her. "You're right. I don't understand."

She sighed and resettled against the wall, looking suddenly exhausted. "I know the difference between a good life and a bad one," she said. "And I'm not willing to go back to a bad one."

"But—"

She shook her head again and they both fell silent. She had canted her head back to catch the sunlight on her face, and he saw her eyes lift and turn to track a silhouette against the sky. He followed her gaze and saw the elongated outline of a blue heron swoop gracefully overhead, circle the cottage once, and head out toward sea.

Then he knew. "Ah."

Geena tilted her head in his direction. "'Ah' what?"

"Bel's a shape-shifter."

She raised her eyebrows in a wide-eyed stare but didn't answer. He worked his way through the clues he hadn't put together until now.

"She's restless—won't stay in one place. That's true of every mystic. She sat on your lap in the form of a cat the first time I met you. She probably takes that shape—or some other animal shape—every day and lurks around the infirmary so she always knows what's happening there. The first time I saw her styled like a woman, I could tell by your expression that you were surprised by something. I'm guessing she ordinarily looks different from the way she's presented herself to me."

Geena's smile was weary but genuine. "Very clever! I do like you."

"Why bother with the disguise? Does no one on the island know she's a mystic?"

She shrugged. "There didn't seem to be a reason to tell them. Yes, we knew Dorrin Isle had brought in mystic healers from time to time—but that didn't mean they were always welcome. Why take chances?"

"Bel must have been in grave danger a time or two, if she's so wary now."

"Her life has been more adventurous than I could describe."

"But even if she wanted to hide the fact that she's a shiftling, what reason would she have for concealing her true face? Forgive me, but there are very few mystics who are so well-known that anyone would recognize them on the streets."

Geena managed a laugh. "No, indeed! Your friends Senneth Brassenthwaite and Kirra Danalustrous might be the only two."

"Then why the pretense?"

"I suppose you would have to ask her."

Something he obviously would never do. He and Geena had struck up a friendship of sorts, but Bel had remained aloof.

"I have a question for you instead," he said. "Why are you willing to die just because Bel's a mystic?"

She was quiet so long, staring at her hands, that he was sure she wouldn't answer. "I apologize," he said. "I know it was rude to ask. But I like you, and I can't stand the thought that you would throw your life away."

She finally lifted her eyes to meet his. Hers were a green so compromised that they looked gray, and in them he read a bitter combination of pain and peace. "I love her," she said simply. "But she's not going to stay. I could feel it a few months ago, that impatience running through her body at night like a wholly unfamiliar type of desire. She loves me, but I'm a weight she doesn't want to carry any longer. I wouldn't say—I would *never* say—she was relieved when I got sick. But I could see her thinking that there was an end to it, a break that she wouldn't have to make herself."

She spread one hand in a helpless gesture. The skin was so translucent that the afternoon sun almost illuminated the individual bones. "I wouldn't have killed myself once she left me, but I wouldn't have wanted to go on living without her. This way, I won't have to."

He came to his knees so he could take her hand in his. A shocking liberty, but her cold fingers clung to his as if grateful for his warmth. How could he argue, how could he insist that her own life had value even if the woman she loved moved on? He was too familiar with the belief that there was no shape to his own life without Kirra to provide the contours. But he couldn't bear to think of Geena tamely submitting to death because the living was just too hard.

"I know," he said. "I do understand. But I think you should try it anyway. Maybe you would find something else to live for. Maybe you would find someone else to love. Maybe you would just travel the countryside, having developed a taste for wandering—not going back to your old unhappy life, but finding an altogether new one. You can always die later, if you decide you want to. But you can't live again unless you take the chance now."

"Dear Donnal," she said, squeezing his hand harder. "Thank you for not offering useless platitudes. I think you are very wise and very kind. But I don't think I can make the effort." She lifted his hand briefly to her cheek; he felt her skin soft and cool against his fingers before she released him. "I'm glad you know everything. It's comforting somehow. But now can you help me inside? I'm so very tired. I might sleep until the end of the world."

Kirra was not only awake and halfway through a meal when Donnal made it back to the barracks, but she fidgeted and squirmed on the hard chair.

"*There* you are," she exclaimed when he strolled in. "Come eat something and then let's go for a walk. I've seen nothing of this island but the path between the infirmary and the cottage. You have to show me all the pretty places."

He slid to a seat across from her and laughed at her peremptory tone. *That* was the old familiar Kirra, impudent and demanding. "Where's the grim exhausted serramarra I've gotten used to?" he teased, accepting a plate from Cloris. "She didn't have the energy to order me around."

She laughed back. "Maybe by practicing so much magic, I'm making myself *stronger*," she said. "You know, the way Justin and Tayse get better at fighting because they train all the time."

"It's never seemed to work that way with magic before."

She finished off a bread roll then reached over to pilfer a slice of his cheese. "What I really think is that the transformation is easier in reverse," she said. "You and I can shift from human to animal and back without any extra effort. But for people who aren't *meant* to be animals, it's much harder to change them in that direction. It's simpler to make them human, because their bodies want to return to their natural states. So it didn't take so much out of me to make Josie a girl again."

"Makes sense," he said, lifting his plate out of reach

before she could steal a small tomato. "Go get your own food."

"But I'm hungry."

"So am I."

"I don't know why. All you do is loll around all day. Or talk to people. *That's* not hard."

"Well, all you do is sleep."

She jumped up. "I'm not sleeping *now*. Let's go exploring."

He crammed a last bite of chicken in his mouth as he rose to his feet and followed her out the door. The air was still comfortably warm, though the breeze drifting in from the ocean brushed their skin with a salty chill. They headed to the beach just as the lowering sun began strewing coins of gold across the wrinkled water. Despite the fact that the sand was littered with rocks and driftwood, Kirra stripped off her shoes to walk barefoot along the tideline.

"Be careful or you'll cut your feet open," he warned.

"I'm changing my soles to hooves," she retorted.

He peered down at the dainty pink toes. "Obviously not."

"Well, I've made them all calloused. You should try it."

"Too much trouble."

She spread her arms wide and spun in one quick pirouette, eyes closed, face lifted to the sun. "It feels so good to be outside! If I wasn't trying to conserve my energy, I'd turn myself into a gull and fly around the whole island."

"You're in a good mood."

She laughed. "I *am!* Donnal, it *worked!* And it was

so *easy!* We saved that girl's life and we're going to save more, and I am so *happy* that the world holds more than war and treachery and heartache—" She fell abruptly silent, perhaps remembering her most recent heartache, and then shook her golden hair back with an air of determined cheerfulness. "Well, it *does*," she said defiantly.

"What's your plan for tomorrow?"

"I know that the parents of the changed children are clamoring to have them back in human shape, but they'll have to wait. It's the sick ones I have to concentrate on now. So I will spend the next few days changing the last patients into puppies so they can start getting treatment. And *then* I'll reverse the spells on the other ones."

"By my count, there are seven who have yet to be transformed. Of those, three might never agree."

"Maybe they'll change their minds. Once they see all those hale and healthy children dashing around the infirmary, gobbling up pastries and knocking over chairs."

He grinned. "I can't see anyone lingering too long once they've been cured. The place will empty out fast."

"You're right," she agreed. "Nona and Carter plan to leave in the morning, and I can't blame them. But that means it'll be another two days before there's a miracle walking around to remind people what magic is capable of."

"It was a big enough miracle," he said. "I think everyone will remember."

"At any rate, if I can only manage two a day, I imagine it might be another couple of weeks before everyone has been changed, and cured, and changed back again."

"What, are you bored already? We've only been here seven days!"

"I'm not bored yet. But three weeks on Dorrin Isle?" She shivered delicately.

"What do you want to do once we're finished here?"

She sighed. "What I *want* to do is roam around the countryside, maybe visit the Wild Mother's temple in Danalustrous, maybe head south or west. What I *have* to do is return to Ghosenhall to meet my father. Apparently, the king has called some convocation and is requiring all the marlords to attend. My father wants me there, so I shall go." She kicked at an incoming wave, sending up a small splash of water. "*We* shall go," she amended.

"Will the others be there?" There was no need to name them. He meant Senneth and Tayse, Justin and Cammon. Their almost constant companions for the past year. Strange to think that, not so long ago, many of them had been strangers to each other.

"It seems likely, though any of them could be gone on commissions for the king."

"And after Ghosenhall?"

She spread her arms again, as if to embrace the entire world. "Wherever we want! We shall go somewhere new every day! So be thinking about where you might want to go."

Wherever you go, he thought. "Anywhere but Gisseltess," he said, and she laughed.

They walked for at least an hour, sometimes talking, sometimes not. It was the longest they had been together in human form—awake—since sometime on the road to Rappengrass. It was easy to slip into the old companionable rhythms, calling up idle memories, pointing out odd features of the landscape, lapsing into silence, then offering up another random observation. Kirra's good mood held, but Donnal could sense she was tiring before she was willing to admit it.

"Time to go back for the night," he said as darkness began swallowing the layered scarlet of sunset.

"Not yet," she said instantly. "I want to see what's on the other side of that cove."

"Go ahead," he replied, turning toward the path that would lead them home. "But I'm heading back."

"Donnal! What if I get eaten by rabid wolves once you've deserted me?"

"I pity the rabid wolf who thinks he can get the best of you."

"Well, but I could get *lost*."

He was already moving away from her; he answered over his shoulder. "I don't think it's possible for anyone to get lost on such a small island."

He heard her make a disgruntled sound deep in her throat, but he also heard her turn to follow him. "*Senneth* wouldn't leave me alone in a strange place."

"Senneth would have abandoned you long before this."

"Wait up, at least."

He did, but they were going uphill and the track was narrow, so she had to trail behind him as they sought their way on the rocky path. There was a particularly tricky stretch over a fall of tumbled boulders, so he took her hand to help her clamber up. She immediately pushed ahead of him to take the lead, and he dropped back a few paces to follow her.

As always.

It was completely dark by the time they rounded the

final curve to their destination, though the cottage was just an inhospitable smudged shape under the night sky.

"How nice it would be to have a candle in the window to welcome us home," Kirra grumbled as she put her hand on the door. "Do we have enough kindling to start a fire?" When he didn't answer, she turned her head to look for him. "Donnal?"

And then she stilled, her hand upraised, her body briefly motionless. The moonlight was just bright enough to strike a faint phosphorescence from her hair. She looked like the memory of a ghost, already dissipating into the night air.

He trotted up beside her on four feet and nudged the door open. He heard her take one long, slow breath before she clattered in behind him.

"Excellent, there's plenty of wood," she said, her voice completely steady. "I do love a fire on a chilly night."

CHAPTER 9

In the morning, Josie and her parents were gone, but the families of two of the remaining patients were already in the dining hall, awaiting the mystic's arrival. The transformations from human to animal were just as draining for Kirra as the previous ones, so Donnal was left on his own once again as she slept away the afternoon.

He made his way to Lilah's room, to find her too weak to sit up. Donnal glanced at Maria, and she met his eyes, her face etched with terror and despair. So it was as it appeared. Lilah was fading quickly.

But her eyes remained interested and alert, and she managed to summon a smile for him as she lay against the pillows. "There you are!" she said, her voice breathy with effort. "I've missed you."

He pulled up a chair beside the bed. "It's been a busy couple of days. I suppose you heard about Josie."

"Nona and Carter brought her to our room," Maria said. "I wouldn't have believed it if I hadn't seen her for myself. Laughing and talking and strong as could be."

"And did that make you think that magic might not be so terrible?" Donnal asked Lilah in a teasing tone.

She pulled the sheets closer to her chin. "Maybe it wasn't terrible to Josie, but it might be for *me*."

"I can think of worse things," Maria said quietly.

"In a few days, the serramarra will be turning two more puppies back to human children," Donnal said. "You'll see how healthy they look. Maybe that will convince you."

Lilah shook her head. "Stop asking me."

No good to upset her with repeated appeals. He changed the subject, recounting stories about Ghosenhall and the young Princess Amalie. Since it was clear she liked hearing about the nobility, he told her a little about Geena, keeping to the less scandalous parts of the tale. "She didn't like her life when she was living in a fine mansion, so she set off to see the world, and she's traveled all over Gillengaria with a friend," he said.

"Is she sad to be dying?" Lilah wanted to know.

"I think she's sad that her life is coming to an end, but happy with how she's spent it," he said. "I think she would have been a lot more sad if she'd never left home. If she'd never gotten a chance to do what she wanted."

Maybe his message was too subtle; Lilah didn't seem to realize it was aimed at her. *You too should take the chance to live while you still can.* She just nodded as her eyelids drooped. "I wish I could meet her," she said through a yawn. "She would be fun to talk to." She still seemed to be mulling that over as she dropped off to sleep.

Maria buried her face in her hands. "She can't have much time left," she said in a choked voice. "I can't bear it. I truly can't."

"Do you think it would do any good if Kirra came to

talk to her? Lilah seems fascinated by the nobility, even if she fears mystics. And Kirra can win over anybody when she wants to."

Maria lifted her head, but her face was desolate. "Maybe. I thought seeing Josie would change her mind but—" She shrugged helplessly.

"I'll go now," Donnal said, coming to his feet. "You need rest as much as she does."

"I don't sleep at all. I just watch her while I still have her."

He didn't know how to answer that. He touched her shoulder and left the room, bowed with a borrowed grief. He wasn't sure even Kirra could coax Lilah to submit to magic. The girl could easily be dead before they left the island.

He didn't have any luck with the next two patients on his list, either. The stern-faced woman with the moonstone necklace wouldn't even allow him to glance inside the room where her grandson lay fevered and unresponsive.

"The Pale Mother will take him in her arms when he passes from this world," she said with a zealot's conviction. "And he will not be tainted by magic when he goes."

The Pale Mother has dealt more death than any mystic you ever dreaded, he wanted to retort, but there was no point to it. He merely nodded and left, slipping downstairs and out the door to let the afternoon breeze sweep away some of his anger and melancholy.

Geena was not sitting on her bench outside when

he made his way up the hill, and he hoped that didn't mean she had deteriorated overnight. He was afraid to knock in case she was sleeping, but maybe he could do something else for her.

Gauging the time by the angle of the sun, he estimated he had at least four hours of daylight left. Within seconds, he had transformed himself into an eagle and flung himself into the hard blue sky. It was good to break free of a landbound tether, to shake off the anxiety and misery of the people below. In animal shape, he remembered he was human, but some of the sharpest emotions were blunted; monumental cares seemed smaller, less urgent, easier to ignore. It was simpler to merely exist, to think of nothing but motion and hunger and the constant need for vigilance. It was possible to just *be*.

He traveled easily to the mainland and the market town he had visited once before. He couldn't find the same fruit merchant, but plenty of other farmers were selling apples and berries, and one enterprising vendor was offering bags full of soft citrus-flavored candies. He had to limit his purchases to what he could carry back, but he couldn't leave such a treat behind.

For the return journey, he styled himself as a particularly large great horned owl, capable of carrying double its own weight. With any luck, no one would notice him and wonder why the nocturnal creature was out during the sunlit hours. The load was heavy, so he resumed his human shape as soon as he cruised across the beach of Dorrin Isle, and he completed the rest of his trek on foot.

He had just laid a bag of apples and a packet of

candies on Geena's front bench when the door opened and Bel stepped outside.

"I thought I saw you through the window," she said. "I see you've brought more gifts. Geena will be pleased at your kindness."

He smiled. "Part kindness and part boredom."

"It's difficult for a mystic to sit still," she said. "As I know."

So Geena had repeated their conversation to Bel. He hadn't been sure she would. He gestured toward the path that led to the top of the hill and they began strolling forward. Not so far that they would lose sight of the cabin, but far enough not to trouble Geena with their voices.

"And yet you have agreed to linger on Dorrin Isle for as long as Geena needs you."

"Harder to do than I thought it would be," she admitted. "At times, especially at night, I can feel my bones shifting without my will, as if to force me into another shape so weightless that it will simply rise and float away."

"What's the longest you've stayed in one place?" he asked. "With anybody?"

She gave the question serious consideration. "Once I was out of my teens, you mean, and able to do with my life what I wanted? A little over two years. And even that short time chafed at me, but I had promised."

It was none of his business, he had no right to say it, but he asked anyway. "And what have you promised Geena?"

She was silent so long he thought he might have offended her, and not unreasonably so. "I never lied to her," she answered at last. "From the beginning, she knew who and what I was. She told me she would be content with six months, if that's what I had to offer."

"I think she said it's been five years now."

She nodded. "Because she was willing to travel. Otherwise, I would have been gone within a year. But I am not meant for staying, even with someone who will make the journey with me."

"Kirra could save her," he said. "But she doesn't want to live without you."

There was a flat, slightly tilted boulder at the top of the rise, invitingly placed to offer a view of the landscape unfolding toward the sea. Bel dropped down to its sun-warmed surface, and Donnal took a seat beside her. She looked half amused and half disdainful.

"So which is it?" she said. "You want me to persuade her to live, even though she will be heartbroken when I'm gone? Or you want me to pretend I will stay so that she takes the cure—and then is devastated when I leave?"

"There's a third possibility."

She shook her head. "There's not. There's a growing wildness in my heart and I am the one who will die if I cannot feed it." She stared at him with an intense expression. "Don't tell me you don't understand what I mean."

"I understand it. I've felt it. Every mystic has."

"And yet I can feel you brimming with disapproval."

"You think ordinary men and women don't feel those same impulses every day—don't fret about their lives and wish they were married to someone else and wish they didn't have to tend the cattle or sow the fields or watch the children? Yet they accept their responsibilities and they stay."

She shrugged. "If they want to go, they should go. No one should let their lives be bounded by the things that smother them."

"You're so selfish," he said.

She flinched back, a flush of anger on her cheeks. "Would you say the same thing to a hawk that killed a rabbit? To a river that flooded its banks? This is how I was made—I cannot be any other way."

"That's an easy excuse," he said. "You don't *want* to be any other way."

"I don't," she snapped. "And I won't apologize for it."

"I just wish that your desire for freedom wouldn't end in Geena's death."

She shrugged again. "And shouldn't she be allowed to make her own choices? Shouldn't she be able to say, 'This is the path I want to take,' even if *you* think her decision is wrong? I might be selfish, but you're arrogant."

"I'm sad," he said. "I have seen too many people sustain too many losses. I want to believe that there are second chances, new opportunities, if only we can hold on long enough. I wish that Geena would be willing to find out what else her world might hold even when you're gone."

"I would wish that for her, too," Bel said. "But I can't open her eyes for her."

"What if it takes her two months to die?" he asked. "Will you stay that whole time?"

"If I have to."

Studying her for a moment, Donnal could see the tension in her shoulders, sense her muscles coiled in protest. He doubted she would be able to bring herself to remain another week, let alone eight or ten. *It's my nature,* she would no doubt tell herself as she winged away one night while Geena lay sleeping. *I can't help who I am.*

"And afterward? Where will you go?"

"Wherever I want." She glanced over her right shoulder, where the coastline lay drowsing in the ancient gold of late afternoon. "Anywhere but Danalustrous."

"Geena said you grew up here. Do you still have family around?"

"I suppose so, though I haven't seen any of them in nearly thirty years. They probably think I'm dead." She must have caught the look on his face, because she laughed. "And don't call me selfish again! I'm sure they were just as glad to see the last of me."

"Because they hated mystics?"

"Because I was difficult and contrary and impetuous and unkind. I don't think the magic bothered them at all."

He tilted his head to regard her curiously. "Geena said you had lived an adventurous life."

"Yes, though I don't intend to regale you with it now," she said. He had ruffled her earlier with his talk of irresponsibility, but she was back in a good humor now. "I have to think you have stories that are just as interesting as mine."

He thought back on the last year, all the dangers he and Kirra had faced as they circled the kingdom with the Riders and their fellow mystics. "Some of them more terrifying than interesting," he said, "and I don't feel like telling them either."

She nodded toward the cottage, where, even from this distance, they could see that Geena had stepped onto the front porch, clad in her habitual blanket. She bent over to sort through the bags Donnal had left behind and straightened up with an apple in her hand. Shading her eyes with her other hand, she gazed up at the sky, as if looking for a hawk or a heron.

"We can swap tales some other time," Bel said, coming to her feet.

Donnal followed suit. "Around a fire some evening," he agreed. "With plenty of wine."

She laughed and headed down the track, Donnal close behind. He was pretty sure both of them doubted they would ever have a private conversation again.

Another night of sleep and silence, Donnal curled at Kirra's feet.

Another day of magic and exhaustion, Kirra slumbering at the infirmary and Donnal looking for ways to fill the hours. This time, after visiting the mainland market, he brought his treasures to Cloris so all the visiting families could enjoy a treat. She was already planning to make a batch of tarts before he'd left the kitchen.

Another night, another dawn. Donnal was outside, stripped to the waist as he washed up at the pump, when Kirra wandered outside.

"You're awake early," he said, toweling himself off.

"I'm excited. Today I get to reverse the spells on two of my patients. It's time for a little more joy, don't you think?"

"Always time for that," he agreed.

Not surprisingly, the dining hall was packed with anyone who was willing to step away from a sickbed to witness more marvels. Benjy and Will were chasing each other around the room, and Cloris scolded them sternly when they almost caused her to trip. Their mothers huddled together in the center of the room, arms around each other for support, too nervous to sit or speak.

Kirra sank gracefully to the floor and clapped her hands. "Here!" she called imperiously. "Enough playing! Time to be little boys again."

They bounded over, frisking around her knees, barking in her face. She laughed and grabbed Benjy when he didn't dart back quickly enough, holding him even though he squirmed to get away. When she leaned in to touch her nose to his, he licked her chin.

"Be still," she whispered. "Be human."

As if hypnotized by her voice, the small wriggling shape grew calm and the dark eyes gazed back at her. The tufted brown fur uncoiled, lay flat, lost its sheen, warmed to a rosy beige with the texture of skin. The body lengthened and bulked up; the face lightened and rearranged itself. The puppy was a child, blinking in shock and wonder. His mother shrieked and dove to the floor to take him in her arms. Everyone else in the room erupted in cheers. Kirra glanced around, looking for Donnal, her eyes ablaze with triumph.

"Well done," he said.

She snapped her fingers to the second dog, and he trotted over, all sleek gold hair, lolling pink tongue, and inquisitive eyes. And minutes later, all tousle-headed boy, open-mouthed and astonished. He put his hands to his cheeks and laughed out loud. His mother was sobbing so hard she couldn't move or speak. But when he jumped up and raced over to throw his arms around her, she cried out his name over and over, as if she had never learned any other form of language. Kirra watched them with a narrow-eyed exultation.

Donnal leaned over to help her to her feet. "Time to rest now," he said.

"No, I feel good—I feel strong. I could do one more."

"No," he said, overriding her. "The strain might hit you later. You know you can manage two transformations. Let it go at that. The others can wait another day."

"But—"

"If you're up to more activity, come visit Lilah and see if you can persuade her to submit to magic."

That appealed to her, as he'd thought it would. But when he led her upstairs to Lilah's room, he thought they might have come too late. The child lay on the bed, thin and shivering, her face colorless. Donnal felt a sense of loss like a hammer to his heart.

Kirra breezed into the room as if she hadn't even noticed its occupant was dying. "You must be Lilah!" she exclaimed. "Donnal has told me about you almost every day and I've been longing to meet you! Is it all right if I sit with you a while?"

Lilah's tired eyes brightened and she managed a smile. "Oh yes!" she said, seeming to speak with an effort. "I wish you would! It's true—you're as beautiful as everyone says."

Casting an anguished look at Donnal, Maria silently scrambled up from her seat by the bed. Kirra took her place, laughing softly.

"My stepmother always told me that only a vain woman cares if she's beautiful, and so I have tried to be witty and charming as well," she said. "But sometimes I feel ugly and dull and very crabby. Do you ever have days like that?"

Lilah managed a breathy laugh. "Yes! It's so funny that a serramarra would feel that way, too."

"So what do you do on the days you feel low?" Kirra asked. "Do you visit your friends? Play with kittens? Sing as loud as you can?"

"I like to read," Lilah said.

"So do I!" Kirra answered. It was a lie, of course; she could barely be bothered to sit still long enough to get through a chapter. "What are your favorite kinds of stories?"

"The ones about people who fall in love."

"Romances! Yes, those are the best."

Lilah grew more animated. "Especially the ones where the prince meets a young beggar girl, and no one believes she's good enough for him, but he marries her anyway."

"Yes! And it's the best decision he ever made because she's good and kind and it turns out that all his subjects love her."

"And she gets to live in the palace and eat whatever she wants and cover herself with jewels."

Kirra leaned forward as if she had just found a kindred spirit. "Do you like jewelry?" she demanded. "I *love* it."

Lilah sighed. "Oh, I do. I don't have any, although my grandmother says she's going to leave me her gold necklace when she's gone. And maybe someday I'll have enough money to buy myself a ring."

"What kind of ring? What sort of stone?"

"A ruby, of course! For Danalustrous."

Kirra half-turned in her chair to look at Donnal. He and Maria had stayed mute and motionless this whole time, not wanting to draw the slightest attention to themselves while Kirra dazzled the dying girl. Now he stepped forward, a questioning lift to his eyebrows. "What?" he asked.

She had her hand out. "Give me something. A belt buckle, maybe."

"Will a button do?"

"Perfect."

He twisted off the flat brass button that held his shirt closed at the throat. Maria had backed herself against the wall mural and watched in bewilderment as he dropped the button in Kirra's palm. She turned back to Lilah.

"They've told you I'm a shape-shifter, of course," she said. "I can take any form I want—but I can turn *things* into other things if I feel like it. Watch." She curled her fingers up just enough to turn her hand into a cup. The dull matte of the humble metal began to shimmer against her skin, taking on a dark sparkle and a smug sheen. Kirra made a fist, then opened her hand again, to reveal a nugget of red set in a simple gold band. She presented it to Lilah with a flourish.

"A ruby ring that I made just for you," she said.

Speechless, Lilah took it from her hand, holding it shakily up to the light. "Is it—is it *real*?"

"As real as anything you'd find in the finest shop."

"And will it—how long will it be like this?"

"I could change it back if I wanted to—but I don't want to. It will be a ruby ring forever."

Lilah darted a look at her mother, as if to make sure that it was permissible to accept such generosity. Maria nodded jerkily. Lilah slipped it on the third finger of her right hand. "It fits!" she exclaimed. "Oh, serra, it's so *beautiful!* Can I really have it?"

Kirra leaned forward and wrapped her hand around Lilah's so tightly that Donnal thought the jewel might be digging into her palm. "I want you to have it," she said. "Something to remember me by."

Unsaid went all the corollaries, but Donnal knew everyone in the room was thinking them. Kirra was clever enough not to frighten Lilah by speaking them aloud. *You will only live long enough to remember me if you allow me to transform you the way I transformed that button. I have showed you what I am capable of. Can you bring yourself to trust me now?*

"Thank you so much," Lilah whispered. "I would never forget you."

Kirra smiled and sat back, still holding Lilah's hand, but Donnal felt a shift in her, a sudden weariness. She might find it easier to return her charges to their human state, but the effort had still been immense. He stepped close enough to touch her shoulder.

"I think you've done enough magic for the day," he said. "You need to come downstairs and nap."

Kirra shrugged away from him. "Not at all! Lilah and I have *much* more to talk about."

He put a hand under her elbow and tugged her away from the bed. "You don't want to collapse on the walk back to the cottage," he said. "And even if *you're* not tired, I think Lilah is."

"I'm not," Lilah said, even less convincingly.

Reluctantly, Kirra released the girl and came to her feet, swaying a little. She stepped back just enough to brace herself against Donnal's chest, and he put his other hand up to steady her. He saw Lilah's eyes, bright with interest, dart from Kirra's face to his.

"We can come back tomorrow," he said. "For now, everybody must rest."

CHAPTER 10

THE NEXT DAY STARTED IN MUCH THE SAME WAY, though fewer people had gathered in the dining hall to watch Kirra's performance. By now, they were all convinced; they were just awaiting their own turns at joy.

The first transformation went smoothly, and soon a boy of about five years old had been swept up in his father's arms and smothered with tears and kisses. But the second conversion took more effort. Donnal could see Kirra's shoulder muscles tighten as her eyebrows drew down in a frown. Her breath came harder and her fingers clenched in a matted weave of brindled fur. He had just enough time to start feeling alarm before some block in the beast's body gave way, and the dog sighed and whined and shifted into the shape of a teenage girl.

But unlike the others who had been brought back to human form, she didn't immediately jump up and burst into a babble of delight and astonishment. She let her mother slip a thin nightgown over her body, but then she lay back on the table, her dark hair spread out behind her, her spindly arms folded across her chest, and her eyes half-closed.

"Doreen?" her mother said in a worried voice, bending over her to brush her fingers down the wan cheek. "Can you talk to me?"

For an answer, Doreen turned to her side, drawing her knees up toward her chest. "It hurts," she moaned.

The half-dozen parents lingering in the room exchanged glances of apprehension as they gathered in a tight knot of worry. Two of them cast looks of suspicion Kirra's way.

Doreen's mother ran her hand down the girl's shoulder and hip. "What hurts? Is it your stomach still?"

Kirra had stepped away when the transmogrification was complete, but now she pushed herself back against the table. "What's wrong?" she asked sharply. Donnal wasn't sure if she was angry or afraid. "Did she have some other illness before she came down with red-horse fever?"

The mother nodded, her eyes never leaving Doreen. "We thought it was just her monthly bleeding, but it never stopped. She was in pain all the time. And when the fever came—we didn't know which one would take her first."

"It would have been useful to know this sooner," Kirra snapped. "The medicines I gave her only treated the fever."

The woman shook her head hopelessly. "I didn't think you could save her anyway," she whispered.

Donnal thought Kirra gentled her voice with an effort. "Maybe I still can. Let me see if I can read the trouble in her body."

Doreen resisted, but Kirra drew the girl's hands away from her abdomen and began pressing gently on the flesh between her hips. The girl made small whimpering sounds but lay passive under Kirra's probing. She had closed her eyes and didn't bother reopening them.

"Yes," Kirra said, her voice low and her face intent. "I can feel it—a growth inside her womb, a sickness, an—I can't explain it."

Doreen's mother covered her face with her hands. "She's going to die, isn't she? I let you turn her into a *dog*, and it did no good, and I can never tell my husband any of it."

Kirra slanted a quick glance at Donnal, and he came forward to gently pull the woman away from the table. "Let Kirra get to work," he said. "She's a healer. She has saved many a sick girl before Doreen."

The woman choked back a sob but allowed him to move her back a few paces. Never lifting her hands from the girl's body, Kirra used her foot to drag over a chair so she could sit beside the table. Everyone else in the room took a few involuntary steps closer, no one speaking or making any other sound. Even the noises from the kitchen had stopped as the workers paused to watch.

Kirra's face was a study in determination; her fingers splayed over Doreen's stomach with a tension that showed the corded sinew. There was no flash of magic, no iridescence sinking from Kirra's hands into Doreen's body, but the room seemed to vibrate with a barely audible hum. Donnal felt the ambient air spark with heat, then dramatically cool. Doreen took a hard sip of air and opened her eyes.

"What did you do?" she whispered.

Her mother tore away from Donnal and flung herself at her daughter. "What? What did she do to you?" she wailed.

Doreen pushed herself up on one elbow. "The pain is better," she said wonderingly. "I feel sore, but I—it doesn't hurt just to breathe."

Now the silent watchers began to rustle and mutter; now Doreen's mother just stared down at her. "Are you—are you *cured*?"

Kirra hadn't exactly slumped over, but Donnal thought only willfulness and pride were keeping her upright. "The malignancy is gone," she said in an exhausted voice. "She'll recover her health. But I doubt she'll ever be able to bear children. I can't be certain, but I think the womb was too damaged."

"But—but she'll live?" Doreen's mother demanded. She sounded dazed. "You're sure?"

Kirra attempted a smile. "The two diseases that brought her here have been chased from her body," she said. "Neither of those things will kill her now."

The woman started sobbing. Doreen sat up and threw her arms around her mother's neck, weeping just as hard. Some of the onlookers were crying, some were smiling, and all of them were watching Kirra with amazement and a touch of fear. *How powerful this mystic is. What else can she do that may not be so generous or kind?*

Donnal tugged her to her feet. "I know, I know," she grumbled. "Sleep now. You're always telling me to sleep." But she leaned on him heavily as he guided her to the little bedroom.

"And you would be wise to do what I say," he answered, helping her into bed.

She caught his hand and nursed it against her cheek. "Dear Donnal," she sighed. "I don't know what

I'd do without you."

He waited the two minutes it took before she was asleep. He thought, *You'll never have to find out.*

Lilah had been waiting for him. She looked even more exhausted than Kirra and even more determined to keep her eyes open.

"I know your secret," she said the minute he stepped into the room.

He raised his eyebrows and glanced at Maria, who smiled and looked away. "I didn't know I had any secrets," he responded.

When she lifted a hand to point at him, he saw the ruby ring flashing on her finger. "You're in love with the serramarra."

"I told her and *told* her it's none of her business," Maria said. "Such a rude little girl! I wouldn't blame you if you turned around and walked out of here right now."

It took him that long to recover from his shock. But he was practiced at hiding his feelings, so he merely smiled and pulled up the extra chair. "I think you've read too many of those romances you talked about," he said.

"It's true. I could tell. The way you looked at her. It's like the prince and the beggar girl, except it's the serramarra and the peasant boy."

"*Lilah!*" Maria was aghast.

"I *am* a peasant's son," Donnal said. "Hardly an insult."

"And you think you're not good enough for her, so

you won't tell her how you feel."

He leaned forward to touch her forehead. "I think you're fevered. Delirious." Her skin felt hot but slightly clammy, and her eyes were overbright. He thought the thrill of her discovery had poured energy into her veins, which would exact a steep price as soon as her excitement wore off.

"She won't stop talking about the serramarra," Maria said.

"Did you like her?" he asked Lilah.

"Oh, she was wonderful! So beautiful and so *kind*."

"I see you're wearing your ruby ring."

Lilah sounded anxious. "I don't have to give it back, do I?"

He laughed. "No! She made it for you. Wasn't that amazing?"

"I never saw anything like it."

"And you weren't afraid, were you, when she showed you her magic?"

"No!"

He leaned closer. "So you wouldn't be afraid if she practiced her magic on you?"

She jerked back against her pillows, her eyes grown suddenly wide. "That's different."

"It's exactly the same thing."

She scrunched her face up. "It's not. Stop asking me. It's *not*."

He put his hands up in a gesture of surrender. "I'm sorry. We can talk about something else."

She hesitated, as if she was about to say she didn't want to talk to him at all, but then she relaxed and nodded. "Tell me about Ghosenhall," she said. "Tell me about Princess Amalie."

He stayed half an hour, relating all the details about Amalie that seemed suitable for repeating, and then sharing what little he knew about Geena when Lilah wanted to know how the other woman was doing. When she seemed to be on the verge of nodding off, he excused himself and came to his feet, promising to return tomorrow.

She didn't answer, so he thought she might already be asleep. He glanced at Maria as he headed to the door, but her gaze was fixed on her daughter's face and she had her arms wrapped around her body as if trying to keep herself from breaking. He wasn't sure she'd succeed.

Kirra's mood was as bleak as Donnal's when she finally woke up late that afternoon. Neither of them could bear the thought of spending another minute inside the infirmary, so they borrowed a basket from Cloris and carried their dinners down to the beach. Kirra flirted her fingers over the sand to create a thick blanket for them to sit on, though Donnal disapproved of her using even that much magic when she was so weary. They didn't talk much as they ate the meal and watched the sun drift toward the horizon.

"You tired yourself out too much," he said, finally breaking the silence. "Healing Doreen on top of changing her back."

"I could hardly let her die after all the trouble I'd already gone to," she said with a touch of humor. She scooped up a handful of sand and let it dribble from her palm. "Besides, it was a disease I knew how to cure. I'd done it once before."

"Really? I don't remember that."

She gave him a fleeting glance and returned her attention to the ocean. There was hardly any breeze tonight, but it still managed to play with the fine golden tendrils framing her face. "You weren't around," she said. "It was in Ghosenhall just a few weeks ago."

When he had been in hawk shape, following her from a distance, unable to leave her, unable to resume his place at her side. He wondered who had benefited from that fortunate bit of sorcery. He said, "I suppose I missed a lot during the last part of the journey."

She nodded vigorously. "Oh, you did! All the action in Rappengrass."

"Saving the marlady's granddaughter."

"That part was marvelous," she said. "But another part was horrible."

He waited to see if she would tell him, and after a long pause, she sighed. "One night I attended a gathering of Thirteenth House lords to see if they were plotting against the king. And my uncle Berric was there. Trying to rouse the others to revolution."

He was stunned. Growing up, Kirra had been exceptionally close to her aunt and uncle, her only remaining ties to her mother. She had always been a little amused at how much they despised her father because they assumed—as anyone who knew him would—that Malcolm had been the reason the marriage failed. "Has Berric been working with the rebels all this time?"

"It seems he has," she said. "And at this little gathering, when I spoke out against the notion of treason, he tried to poison me."

"He *what*?"

She glanced at him, then back at the sea. "I'd taken the shape of someone else, so he didn't recognize me." She took a deep, shuddering breath. "But I didn't recognize him, either, because he'd also taken an unfamiliar form."

He gave her a sharp look. "I thought he didn't have any magic."

"That's what he always told me," she said tiredly. "But it was a lie. Everything he ever said to me was a lie. I thought he loved me, and instead he was trying to destroy everything I loved."

He touched her fleetingly on the wrist, not sure he could bear to take her in an embrace, not sure she would welcome his arms around her. "I'm so sorry," he said. "Such an unimaginable loss."

"Tayse sent him back to Ghosenhall for the king to deal with, even though I thought my father should be the one to handle him," she said. "My father always loathed Berric, and I never understood why."

"Maybe Berric reminded him of your mother."

She shook her head. "My father never hated her. I doubt he ever actually loved her, either. He has always cared about Casserah and me more than he cared about any of his wives. Because we are part of Danalustrous and Danalustrous is all that matters to him in the world."

"I am sure your uncle loved you, too," he said. "In some fashion."

"Maybe. I'm not sure it matters, because how can I love *him*? How can anybody love anyone? Some days the world seems like nothing but a web of secrets and betrayals."

"You know that's not true," he said. "Justin and Tayse—all the Riders—they are loyal to the core. Senneth would never abandon you. Your sister will cling to you till the end of the world."

He couldn't bring himself to add *And I will never leave you*, because she could have only one reply. *You did once*. And what could he say to that? *You were the one who broke the unspoken covenant.* Theirs was an impossibly complex and delicate relationship. They owed each other too much; they had promised each other nothing. They were so intertwined they could never be separate, and they were so far apart they could never be together.

The silence hung between them for a moment, and then Kirra sighed again and resettled herself on the sand. "And we'll never get Cammon out of our lives," she said with an attempt at lightness. "He's inescapable."

"But I'm sorry about Berric."

"I'm sorry about so many things," she said. She spread her hands and stretched them toward the horizon, as if trying to snag the last drops of sunlight with her fingertips. "But I'm glad I've come to Dorrin Isle. If I can't heal my own heart, maybe I can heal someone else's. Maybe that rights the balance in the world."

He stood up and took her hand, tugging her to her feet. "When *you* turn philosophical, it's time to get you home," he said. "Come on. There will be much to do tomorrow."

"Yes," she said. "I'm looking forward to another burst of joy."

CHAPTER 11

But joy had been supplanted by grief be-fore they even made it to the infirmary in the morning. Eileen met them at the cottage door to tell them one of the patients had died overnight.

Donnal felt a stab of fear so intense it was physically painful. "Lilah?"

"No. A young boy—here with his grandmother, who's covered with moonstones and practically spits every time she sees the serramarra."

Relief bowed his head, and he felt a moment's shame for that. Every life was equally sweet; each death was to be equally mourned. "It's terrible news," he said.

"One of the men is going to row her—and the body—over to the mainland by noon. She doesn't want to delay, and I can't blame her. I thought it might be best if you stayed away until she's gone."

"Of course," said Kirra. "Let us know when we should make an appearance."

So the morning was excruciating and the afternoon was solemn. Only the parents of the changed children presented themselves for the ritual of reversing magic, and while it was clear they felt both gratitude and jubilation, their celebrations were muted and private.

"It's getting emptier here all the time," Cloris remarked as she brought them a plate of apple tarts afterwards. "We used to have fifty or seventy people here at a time, and now there are only a few families left, all just waiting their turns to go home. Soon there won't be any work left for me to do."

"I'm sorry to put you out of a job," Kirra said.

Cloris laughed. "Well, my husband will be glad to have me back home! He hates tending the garden and the chickens. And I can't say I'll be sorry that I'm not watching babies die every month. These have been the best two weeks of this whole wretched business."

Kirra smiled tightly and stood up. "I am going to break with tradition and go back to the cabin for my afternoon nap," she said. She touched Donnal's shoulder. "You stay here. I'm fine by myself."

Clearly she wanted solitude, so he watched her go and restrained the impulse to run after her to be sure she made it safely to the cottage. He helped Cloris clean the kitchen, then headed upstairs.

Cloris was right; he hadn't registered it before, but many of the rooms now stood empty. Only nine patients remained in the barracks—eight of them still in animal shape, and one of them human.

When he arrived at Lilah's room, the door was shut. He knocked softly, prepared to walk away if no one answered, but a minute later Maria opened it and stepped out into the hallway. Her face was haggard and her hands were shaking. It was clear she had not slept for at least a day and was bracing herself for calamity. She held her hands out almost blindly and

Donnal took them in a tight clasp.

"She's so sick," Maria whispered. "She keeps coughing and she won't eat anything and I can't think—I can't believe—she can only have a few more days left, and what am I going to *do*? I can't lose her but I'm going to. I don't know how I can go on."

"Is she awake? Can I talk to her?"

Maria nodded.

"You go down to the kitchen," he said gently. "Get something to eat. Have some tea. I'll stay with Lilah until you come back."

She nodded and stumbled away, brushing a hand against the wall to keep her balance. Donnal steadied himself and stepped inside.

Lilah was a small shape on the bed, her dark hair the only bit of color against the white pillows and sheets. She didn't open her eyes until he took the seat beside her and said her name.

Then she looked at him and attempted a smile. "Donnal."

"It seems like you're feeling worse," he said.

"A little."

"You don't have to talk if it makes you too tired. I just wanted to sit with you a while."

She nodded and was silent a moment, but her eyes remained open. "Did you hear?" she said at last. "The boy down the hall died last night."

"I know."

"He was only three. Too young to die."

He brushed her hair from her forehead. Her skin was burning. "You're only fourteen."

"My mother said his grandmother wouldn't let Kirra

near him because she hates mystics."

"I suppose you can understand that."

She moved her head uneasily. "I don't *hate* them. I'm just afraid of magic."

"More afraid of magic than you are of dying?"

She made a sound that was almost a whimper. "How can I let her turn me into an animal? What would I do? What would I think? I wouldn't be *me*."

"Yes, you would. You would know who you are. You would recognize your mother and me and Kirra and everybody. Things would look different, they would *feel* different, but you would still be Lilah."

"What if I couldn't breathe? Just thinking about it makes me feel like I'm drowning."

"I take animal shape all the time and I can breathe just fine."

"What if I die?"

He had to say it out loud. "You know you're going to die if you don't do it."

She started crying and he leaned forward and put his arms around her hot, sticklike body. She flung her hands around his neck and drew him closer. "I know!" she sobbed. "I can't—but I don't want to—but my mother—but Donnal, I'm so afraid!"

"What I'm afraid of is what will happen if you don't let Kirra save you."

"Could you do it? Could you do the scariest thing ever in the whole world?"

"Right now, I'd do anything you asked if it would save your life. Even if I was terrified."

She sniffled and swallowed and drew back enough to look him in the eyes. Their faces were only inches apart. "Would you tell Kirra you loved her?"

He stared at her and could not speak.

Her thin fingers tightened on the back of his neck. "*Would* you? Isn't that what you're most afraid of?"

His body felt as fevered as Lilah's; his skin was just one breath away from combusting. He was as dizzy as a small bird buffeted by a capricious wind, he was as hollow as an aged and abandoned bone.

Could he? Barter his heart to ransom the life of a stranger? Peel away every last defense, expose every comforting pretense, strip his heart naked and never know peace again?

"And if I did?" he whispered. "Would you allow her to change you?"

"Yes."

He rested his forehead against hers. Kirra's words echoed and rearranged themselves in his mind. *If I shatter my own heart, maybe I can restore someone else's. Maybe that rights the balance in the world.*

"Then I will."

Donnal's blood was racing and he had to fight to keep his breath even as he arrived at the cottage door. He had no idea how he would start this conversation, no idea what he would say. He had tried, on the short journey, to fashion his opening sentences, but his mind was an absolute blank.

But he had promised.

But he thought he might die.

"Kirra?" he called, stepping inside. There was no

answer and he realized, with a drenching rush of relief, that he had earned a reprieve: She was not there. A temporary delay. But maybe it would give him time to marshal his wits.

Cloris had sent him home with supper for both of them, so he set it up on the sideboard, then took some time to tidy the small space and pump fresh water. Still, these tasks didn't take long, and as the minutes ticked by, he grew concerned. Where had she gone? Had she sought to soothe her troubled soul by taking the shape of a gull and winging across the ocean, as far as she could fly from the turmoil and trouble of men? What if she had misjudged her strength, what if she had been unable to make it back to land? Less calamitous but just as possible, what if she had gone rambling across the island, setting her face toward the sea breeze in the hope it would scrub away her darkest thoughts? What if she had fallen, or twisted her ankle, or hit her head? Kirra was a healer, but he wasn't sure she could mend herself. He had never seen her try.

He was just about to go out on reconnaissance when the door opened and Kirra stepped in. He felt his skeleton turn to water.

"There you are," he said, trying to speak lightly. "I was starting to worry."

Her own voice seemed strained, as if she too spoke with an effort. "I was just out wandering," she said. "I have been feeling very cooped up lately. The only places I go are the infirmary and this house, and all I do is eat and sleep."

"And heal people."

"Less than half an hour of my day."

"You're feeling bored?"

"On edge." As if to demonstrate, she began pacing through the small space. "But I realized this morning that we'll be able to leave in four days. There are only eight more children to change back to human shape, and then we can go."

"You might have to linger another week," he said softly. "Lilah has agreed to undergo a transformation."

Kirra halted in mid-stride, her face a study in amazement and delight. "She *has*? That's marvelous! How did you change her mind?"

"We struck a deal. She asked me to do something for her, and I said I would."

Now Kirra's expression changed to something he couldn't read. "And that's all it takes?" she said, a trace of acid in her voice. "I wish I'd known."

His astonishment was so profound that he could only stare. The sun was so low and the windows were so small that the failing gold of twilight left her half in shadow; she appeared to be nothing more than the misty manifestation of a woman. Finally, he managed, "When have you ever asked me for something and I refused?"

She shook her head impatiently and resumed her pacing. "Never. But maybe because I never asked. Maybe because I was afraid to ask."

"Kirra—"

She shook her head again. "Never mind. Are you hungry? It looks like someone brought dinner."

He moved to intercept her, and she came to a dead halt three feet from him. Her eyes were trained on her feet. "Kirra," he repeated. "What are you trying to say?"

She made a clumsy gesture. "It's too hard!" she burst out. "All of this! You're here but you're farther away from me than you've ever been, and I don't know how to get back to where we were." He opened his mouth and she hurried on before he could speak. "And it's my fault—I understand it's my fault—all I have done in the past few months is hurt everyone I touched. I know I broke your heart and I'm sorry, I'm so sorry. And it doesn't matter that my own heart is broken, that's what I deserve, but it's so *hard*. I don't know how long I can go on the way we are now."

Minutes before, she had been frantically pacing, but now she was still, as if a single forward motion would shatter her bones in her body. He stood equally motionless, afraid to step closer, unable to step back.

"Do you want me to leave?" he said in the quietest voice he could muster and still be heard.

"*No!*"

"Then what do you want from me?"

Now she raised her head—flung her arms out—but remained rooted to the spot. "*I don't know!* I've never known! At first, we were just children, we just *existed*. I didn't think about what would happen as we got older and I had to play the part of the noble serramarra. You were always just *there*. And then I started attending the balls and the dinners, and you couldn't follow me, and it seemed like something we had always known and it seemed like it wouldn't matter.

"And I was living two lives side by side. I was the daughter of Malcolm Danalustrous and I knew how to play that part. I would flirt with the men and gossip with the women and wear jewels and gowns and satin slippers. But I was also the shiftling mystic, hunting for my food and sleeping in the forest and taking any shape I liked. I loved both lives. I didn't think I would have to choose between them."

"And I always knew you would."

She shook her head. "No, but you see, I thought I could have them both. I knew my father hoped I would marry an ally for Danalustrous, and I suppose I always vaguely thought I would do it—sometime, not now, not while I still had such a vagabond soul, but *sometime*. I assumed it would be a marriage of convenience and that I would be the lady of the manor when I was required to play that role. Maybe I would provide my husband with heirs—I hadn't really thought it through. But I didn't think I'd have to give up the other half of my life. I thought I could slip away, now and then, run free for a week or a month or a year. I *believed* that." She made a small sound that was almost a laugh. "When I say it out loud, it sounds so stupid."

"My guess is that very few men, even those who are most tolerant of magic, would be agreeable to that arrangement."

Now she met his gaze. In the dim light, her blue eyes looked almost gray. "Whenever I pictured that life—those months when I stepped away from my marriage to roam the kingdom—I always pictured you at my side. I suppose no husband would have allowed that, either."

He returned her regard as steadily as he could. "And when I pictured you married?" he said. "I tried to imagine myself somewhere in your life. Your groom or your courier, perhaps—the person you trusted to take messages to your father or the king. Now and then you might ask for my advice. I would follow you on my own horse, when you went out riding, and if you traveled to another manor house, I'd take hawk shape to guard you on your journey. I knew your life would be completely different, but I thought that I would still be in it."

"And then I met Romar Brendyn."

He nodded. "And everything changed."

For a long moment, silence lay between them. "I can't pretend I didn't love him," Kirra said finally, her voice very low. "I can't say I've stopped loving him. I might love him my whole life."

"But you can't have him."

"I could," she whispered. "I could meet him for stolen nights anywhere in Gillengaria. I can take any shape, I can travel any distance, I can find him in any room—and he would want me there. He loves me, too. It's wrong, of course, I know it's wrong, but I tell myself it's not so terrible. Who doesn't have affairs? What king or queen—what marlord or marlady—has been faithful for a lifetime? I could *have* him even if I couldn't *marry* him."

She paused briefly, then spoke again, even more slowly. "But I *could* have married him," she said. "His wife came to me in Ghosenhall—sick with an illness that I knew how to cure—and asked me if I would heal her. All I had to do was withhold my magic. She would have been dead before the year was out."

He felt his body cased in ice, then licked with flame. It was impossible to speak.

"I saved her. I sent her back to him. And I left him."

He took a long, long breath. "Because you're not selfish enough to be that cruel," he said. "Because, despite your wild heart, you are generous and kind."

"Because, despite how much I loved him, I have a wild heart," she corrected. "He needed a woman who would stay, and I could never be that woman."

"And now you will be in mourning for the rest of your life."

"A part of me, yes, I think so. But I will learn to live without him." Her own breath came slow and shuddering. "But I know I cannot learn to live without you."

The world grew deafeningly silent.

The only sound was Kirra's voice, halting and uncertain. "There is nothing I can offer you. Nothing I can promise you. Nothing I can even ask of you, because I have so little to give in return. I can't abandon my heritage—I'm not like Senneth, I can't renounce my House and my responsibilities. And I could never drag you into that world, force you to undergo the stares and whispers of every noble in Gillengaria."

She came a step closer, another step, close enough to lay her hand with shocking timidity on his arm. He felt the heat of that touch through his sleeve, through his skin, to the copper filaments of his veins. "But I cannot bear to lose you from my life," she said, and if the rest of the world had not been so still, he would not have been able to hear her words. "I don't know who I am if you're not beside me. Can we try—is there a way—is there some kind of life we can live together?"

His own voice was nothing but a choked sound; he couldn't possibly have managed whole words. He swept her into an embrace, and she broke down sobbing against his chest. It shouldn't have felt so new, this sensation of holding her in his arms. They had slept beside each other, leaned against each other, curled up together for heat or comfort more times than he could possibly count.

But it was different this time, charged with such energy the air around them seemed lambent; he felt a sensation like lightning run up his skin. She was leaning into him, she was clinging to him. Her arms tightened around his waist as if she could not draw him close enough. He finally found his voice, but all he managed to say was her name. *Kirra, Kirra, Kirra*. A prayer, a confession, a promise, a revelation. *Kirra, Kirra, Kirra*.

She lifted her head, and even in the near darkness, he could see her face streaming with tears. It was the most natural thing in the world to lean forward, to press his lips against hers, something he had only ever done once before. Again, he felt a thrill of shock that brought every nerve in his body to high alert. He kissed her again.

"I love you," he said. "Maybe you can't live without me, but I don't think I exist without you. I have never expected to have you, but I will never be able to leave you. Take what you want from me and give me back whatever you can. There's nothing else in the world that matters."

"Nobody should make a bargain like that," she whispered against his mouth. Her arms were wrapped so tightly around him she almost could not get enough air to speak. "It's completely unfair to you."

"I don't care."

Now she lifted her hands to press them to either side of his face. He thought she might remold his cheekbones, recolor his skin. He wondered if he would recognize himself the next time he found a mirror.

"I swear I will be better to you from now on," she murmured. "I will try so hard not to hurt you. I'll be so careful! You'll hardly know me, I'll be so good."

He pressed his mouth to hers again. "All you have to be is Kirra. That's all I've ever wanted."

She linked her hands behind his head and pulled him more insistently into the kiss. It was hard to say which one of them began edging the other toward the pallet laid out before the fire, but it was just moments before they had collapsed onto the shallow bed. In between kisses, they wrestled with their clothes, helping each other with the buttons, tugging off shirts and skirts and tossing them aside, until they were both entirely naked.

"Very nice," Kirra said, running her fingertips with a sensuous pleasure across his chest and ribs. "Beautiful muscles, beautiful skin."

He found it in him to laugh, and he returned the favor, stroking his hands down her curves from her collarbone to her hips. "Beautiful skin, beautiful body," he responded.

She turned to her side and pulled him next to her so they were face-to-face on the flat pallet. She draped one arm over his shoulders, hooked her leg over his thigh and drew him closer. "All those years sleeping together," she said, mischief in her voice, "yet this time feels so different."

He flipped her to her back and lowered himself over her. "Very different," he agreed.

She kissed him again and whispered, "But I like it."

It should have been awkward, it should have been

clumsy, and yet they moved together with a familiar ease. Their bodies knew each other so well, every shape, every position; they had always been able to communicate without words. A touch here, a caress there, her hand following his cues, his mouth tracing the contours of her skin. A startled gasp of breath, a crescendo of greed and motion, a strangled moan, a cry, a glorious release. They lay together, panting, smiling, still intertwined and watching each other by the building moonlight.

"Maybe it wasn't such a terrible day," Kirra said at last, "if it was going to end this way."

He laughed and kissed her nose. "I'd suffer any number of awful years if it meant I could have this one night."

"Oh, believe me," she said, "there will be more nights like this."

He gathered her closer in one bone-cracking hug. "But for now, you have to rest. You have to sleep. You have to be strong enough to transform Lilah tomorrow."

"Can I ask?" she said. "What did you promise her to make her agree?"

He started laughing, low and helpless.

"What? What?" she insisted. "Can't you tell me?"

"She said she would allow you to change her—something that absolutely terrifies her—if I would do something that terrifies me."

"I can't imagine what."

"I had to tell you that I loved you."

She stared, then snorted, then started laughing in return. "So I didn't even need to beg you to forgive me!" she exclaimed. "All my abject apologies for nothing!"

He wrapped his arms more tightly around her. "I don't remember any begging," he said. "Or apologies, come to think of it. But I do admit everything you said made it easier for me to say the words."

She snuggled against him. "Well, you kept your promise to Lilah and now I want you to make one to me."

"Anything."

"Don't change. Be Donnal. Tonight and all night and tomorrow. I have missed you so much."

There was only one possible answer to that. He buried his face in her hair. "I love you."

CHAPTER 12

Maria was waiting for them outside of Lilah's room. Her face was creased with anxiety, and every muscle in her body seemed tightly bunched, but she relaxed slightly as she caught sight of Kirra and Donnal. "I'm so glad you're here," she said.

Donnal hurried forward. "Is she worse?"

"I think so, yes. She woke up this morning and took a few sips of water, but she's sleeping again. I hope—I hope—"

Kirra touched her lightly on the shoulder as she stepped past. "It's not too late," she said. "You'll see."

Donnal was pierced by doubt as he followed Kirra inside to find Lilah motionless on the bed. The child was so thin and so quiet that her body could have been nothing more than wadded-up sheets under a rumpled coverlet. He had to swallow a soft exclamation of dismay.

But Lilah's eyes opened when Kirra dropped to the chair beside her bed. "Look at you!" Kirra said in a cheerful voice. "Sleeping the day away! And it's going to be *such* a big day for you!"

Lilah licked her lips with a tongue that seemed thick

and uncooperative. "Did he tell you?" she whispered.

Kirra laughed and leaned down to murmur something in Lilah's ear. The girl managed a smile as she cut her eyes in Donnal's direction.

"Is that good enough for you?" Kirra demanded. "Now will you keep *your* half of the bargain?"

Lilah nodded, but her eyes were still on Donnal. "I'm afraid," she said, still in that wispy voice. "Will you hold my hand?"

He gave up all notion of decorum and settled on the bed right next to her, reaching under the tangle of sheets to free her arm. Her fingers were warm and dry, thin as winter twigs. "Of course I will."

"I suppose I should take off my ruby ring," she said.

Kirra held out her hand. "Give it to me and I'll set it right here on the table. It'll be waiting for you in a week when you're human again."

Lilah complied. "What do I have to do now?"

"Nothing," said Kirra. "Just lie there like a pampered princess while I do all the work."

That made Lilah giggle, though the sound was faint and exhausted. "All right. I'm ready."

Kirra leaned forward, resting the heels of her hands on Lilah's collarbones and cupping her fingers around the scrawny throat. Donnal felt Lilah's hand clench on his as her eyes widened with fear.

"Look at me," he said. "I'll tell you what's happening. You feel that? Those are your bones shifting, shrinking down because you're going to be a lot smaller now. Your muscles might be curling in a little, and you can probably feel your heart beating faster. My face might look a little strange, too—that's because dogs don't see the same way. There won't be as much color in the world. But isn't it amazing how much you can smell? Can you tell that I have a different scent from Kirra and from your mother? Can you guess what they're cooking downstairs for lunch? Oh, and now your skin is changing! It's all fluffing up with fur, and it's so pretty, black and brown with a white blaze on your forehead. But your eyes are the same. Your eyes are pure Lilah." Her thin hot hand had turned into a small rough paw, and he squeezed it tightly. "And that's it. You're done."

Cautiously, the dog lifted her head from the pillow to look around the room. She seemed to be struggling to reposition herself, so Donnal helped her roll to her stomach, though she made no attempt to push herself to a sitting or standing position. She was still gazing about her as if she was trying to adjust her senses to her new reality, as if she was dizzy, or lost, or too sick to make sense of the world.

Kirra pushed her chair back. She was smiling, though with something of an effort; the transformation had had its usual draining effect. "That could hardly have gone better," she said. "What an adorable little creature you are."

Maria was instantly at the bedside, a bowl in her hands. She must have fetched it from the kitchen as soon as Cloris arrived in the morning. "And that's it? Can she start taking the medicine now?"

"Let me give it to her," Donnal said, and Maria passed the bowl to him. It was filled with a thick paste about the color and consistency of oatmeal. He used his fingers to scoop out about a tablespoon. "Here you go," he said.

"You need to eat all of this so you can start to get well."

Lilah obediently licked the paste from his fingers, so he measured out another portion. A third time, a fourth, until the bowl was empty and she was yawning, her tongue a curl of pink inside her pointed mouth.

"Good girl," he said, patting her head. He saw a faint movement under the sheets as she wagged her tail. "You rest now. I'll come back this afternoon to see how you're doing."

"You'll already be feeling better by then," Kirra promised. She stood up a little shakily. Donnal was instantly on his feet to support her.

"What else do I need to do?" Maria said.

"Give her more of the potion every two hours," Kirra said. "Encourage her to drink water and eat. She'll want to sleep for a while, but I'm guessing by tomorrow or the day after, you won't be able to keep her in bed."

"I can't believe it," Maria whispered. "Thank you isn't—there are no words—"

Kirra gave her an impulsive hug. "And while you're taking care of Lilah, you should take care of yourself, too," she suggested. "*You* sleep. *You* eat. You want to be well enough to enjoy the miracle."

Maria nodded, hugged Donnal in turn, then lay down beside Lilah on the bed. The dog leaned forward to press her dark nose against her mother's cheek. The sound Maria made might have been a laugh, might have been a sob. Might have been both.

Donnal tugged Kirra from the room and shut the door quietly behind them. She still seemed unsteady, but her face showed excitement under the weariness. "We did it! We saved her!"

He kissed the top of her head. "*You* saved her."

"A girlish sense of grand romance saved her," Kirra amended with a laugh.

He kissed her again. *Healed by love*, he thought. The only potion in the world that never failed.

Kirra managed one more transformation, turning a sleek, sinewy white terrier into a nine-year-old girl with huge eyes and an infectious smile. She was too weary to perform the second promised reversal of the day, though she apologized profusely. The father was angry, though he tried to hide it, but the mother pressed her hand to her heart and spoke with complete earnestness.

"We're happy to wait another day if it means Lilah will have a chance to live," she said.

"I'm so sorry," Kirra said again. "I'm just too tired."

Kirra stumbled to the small bedroom where she had spent so much time, while Donnal fetched her a glass of water. She sat up just enough to gulp down half of it, then sighed and settled back on the pillow. "I feel so pathetic," she grumbled. "Magic shouldn't take such a toll. *Senneth* never runs out of energy."

"Senneth gets headaches that leave her useless for days," he said. "Everything has its price." He stroked her hair. "Now get some rest."

She caught his wrist. "Stay with me?"

"On this tiny bed?"

"I'll scrunch up really small."

He grinned and freed his hand. "I'm not the one who's exhausted. Go to sleep."

"But it doesn't feel *right* when you're not next to me."

He kissed her cheek and stood up. "I'll be there tonight," he promised.

She pouted, but she didn't have the strength to argue. It was only another minute or two before she drifted off.

He made his way out of the barracks and toward the beach, altering his body before he was even halfway to the water. Gull shape, eminently suited to this terrain and these ceaseless, careless breezes. High above the land, above the ocean, in the great grand emptiness of air.

He needed the expansive space, he needed the rush of wind; his thoughts were too huge and too chaotic to be confined to an earthbound plane. *Kirra loved him.* She had said so, when they had woken up at midnight, starved for food, starved for conversation, starved for touch. She had said it again in the morning, as they lay still deliciously intertwined on that low, uncomfortable, infinitely enchanted bed. Sunlight had painted her skin with radiance, woken the faintest auburn streaks in her golden hair. *I love you. I cannot live without you.*

It seemed impossible that he was living in the same world he had always inhabited. It was as if he had blundered through some hidden door to find himself in another setting altogether, staring at vistas he had never even imagined, all soaring heights and limitless horizons and coruscating stars. He was breathing air dusted with crushed diamonds, scented with starlight and wonder.

Or maybe he was the thing that had transmogrified. The world was the same as it had always been, but he was a different creature entirely. He might look no different, but every particle in his body had metamorphosed. His blood was lightning, his bones were crystal, his heart a geysering fountain. It was not possible to feel so transcendent and still be human. But even though he had taken every shape it had ever occurred to him to try, he could not identify what he had turned into now.

He did not think even the sky could contain his reverent elation.

Hunger eventually drove Donnal back to land, though he remained in the form of a gull as he scavenged for food along the beach. As soon as he was satisfied, he flung himself aloft again, circling the island again because only motion could quiet the clamor in his brain.

Finally, by late afternoon, he started sobering up from his drunken euphoria, so he headed back toward the barracks. He had canted over onto one wing to begin a spiraling descent when he found himself over the small cottage with the blue shutters. A tall, thin figure was hobbling around the perimeter of the house, leaning on a cane and pausing to lift her face toward the sun. Donnal skimmed low enough to see that it was Geena. He dropped swiftly to the ground, changing to human shape as his feet touched the grass.

Geena sensed motion behind her and turned in his direction, smiling as soon as she recognized him. "I didn't see you coming up the path," she said as he approached her. "You must have been in some other incarnation."

"I've been flying all afternoon," he said.

"A pretty day for it."

"A pretty day for a walk," he said pointedly. "I don't think I've ever seen you up and moving around. You must be feeling better."

She nodded. "Every once in a while, I have these bursts of vitality. Fewer all the time, but this morning when I woke up, I could tell it would be a good day. I've been poking around all morning. Wishing I'd started a garden so I could do something useful like pull weeds or pick flowers."

"I could carry you down to the beach so you could wade in the surf."

She looked doubtful. "I've lost weight, but I might be heavier than you realize."

He laughed. "I'd take the shape of a pony," he said. "You could ride in style."

"No, I'm starting to tire. But thank you for the lovely thought."

He glanced around. "Next time you're having a good day, you should ask Bel to take you down to the ocean."

A shadow crossed her face. She gestured toward the wooden bench, and they settled on it side by side. "I'm not sure that's something Bel would enjoy."

An odd thing to say. What woman would not want her ailing beloved to enjoy a rare day of sunshine and sweetness? He tilted his head and waited for her to explain.

"She tries to hide it, but I can tell Bel is dismayed on the days I seem unexpectedly strong."

"That makes no sense."

"I think she's afraid I'll never die and she'll be stuck here forever."

Rage punched him in the chest; it was hard to hide his reaction. "Even for a mystic who values her freedom, that seems exceptionally cruel."

"Not cruel," Geena said. "Simply who she is."

"All of us could excuse our most offensive actions if we used that argument. 'That's just who I am.'"

Geena smiled sadly. "And don't you think all of us do exactly that? I have done things that weren't pretty. I have hurt people I claimed to love. Sometimes I felt as if I had no choice, but of course I did. I wanted to be happy. So does Bel." She shrugged. "And I want her to be happy, too."

"Maybe I shouldn't ask, but do you think she'll stay until the end?"

Geena shook her head. "I thought so when we first arrived, but I don't believe it anymore." She glanced around. "In fact, I'm not entirely certain she's still here. I haven't seen her since this morning."

"Geena—"

She held up a hand to forestall him. "No recriminations, please. You can't change her, and I don't want to."

He bit back the bitter words and tried to find something gentler to say. "And once she goes? Will you return to the mainland to spend your final days with family?"

"I doubt it. The thought of the journey seems so exhausting. I'll just stay here and hope the islanders will care for me. It's a peaceful place, don't you think? It will be easy to slip away."

He couldn't resist reaching over to take her hand. It was astonishing to him how bold he had become at offering physical comfort to people who were nearly strangers. He was usually much more reticent, even with people of his own station, and he was pretty sure the only high nobles he had ever touched were Kirra and Senneth. But here on Dorrin Isle, there had been such bottomless wells of grief, such profound conditions of pain, that all distinctions of class had been leveled. It was not impertinent to offer consolation; it was unkind to withhold it.

"You realize there is another option."

She squeezed his hand. "Not for me," she replied.

He knew he shouldn't press, but he did anyway. "There's a little girl—Lilah, maybe you know about her. When we first arrived, she wouldn't agree to a transformation, but this morning she submitted to Kirra's magic. In a week, she'll be well. A week."

"Wonderful! I'm so happy for her and her family!" Geena exclaimed. "What are they like?"

"Farmers from Danalustrous. Maria—her mother—is so strong and patient and determined. You can tell she has fought hard for everything she's ever loved. And Lilah, she reminds me so much of my little cousin. Interested in everything, in every*body*. I told her about you once, and now she asks about you all the time."

"Oh, that's charming. Tell her I want to know all about her, too."

"All you really need to know is that she finally agreed to be cured."

"Why do you think she changed her mind?"

"Because I made her a promise. If she would do that for me, I would do something for her."

"Isn't that lovely!" Geena said. "What was the promise—no, don't tell me. It is so much more delicious not to know."

"Good, because I wasn't going to tell you, anyway." He smiled as he said it, but he instantly grew serious. "I would do something for you if you would make the same bargain. Just tell me what you want from me."

She lifted his hand to her mouth, kissed his knuckles, and released him. "Dear Donnal," she said. "Just have the grace to let me go."

CHAPTER 13

THE NEXT FEW DAYS WERE THE EASIEST AND dullest of their time on the island. During the first three days, Kirra obediently limited herself to changing back two children at a time, which left her with enough energy to be bored and irritable. Most afternoons, they headed down to the beach so she could walk off her restlessness before dropping to the sand with a sigh of contentment.

They never made it twenty feet from the barracks before Lilah dashed out to accompany them, and once they were at the water's edge, she would dart in and out of the waves until she was soaked to the skin. Donnal usually took his own familiar shape of a black dog and chased her across the shifting sand. When they were both tired out, they would trot over to where Kirra waited and curl up on either side of her, resting their heads on her knees.

Kirra would take Lilah's muzzle in her hands and count down the remaining time. *Two days gone, five days left. Three days gone, four days left.* Lilah always listened closely, then offered one quick, sharp bark. Five minutes later, she would be racing through the surf again.

"When the two of you aren't around, she goes scampering up to Geena's cottage," Maria told them on that third afternoon. Like her daughter, Maria was looking livelier and stronger with each passing day. Her eyes were bright and her laugh was frequent and her face had lost that haunted, exhausted look. She had spent some time adding a portrait of a small white dog to the mural in Lilah's room, and she frequently had streaks of paint on her fingers. "I hope Geena doesn't mind! I don't have the nerve to go up and ask her."

"You should go. She'd like you," Donnal told her.

"Me talking to a Thirteenth House lady! I don't think so."

"Maybe when Lilah is a little girl again," he said.

On the fourth day, only one puppy required transformation, and Kirra was about to claw her way out of her own skin.

"Let's go over to Danalustrous for a few hours," she demanded. "I need something to occupy my time."

"I suppose we could stay on the mainland for a couple of days," Donnal said. "Just come back when Lilah's week is up."

Kirra briefly considered the idea before shaking her head. "She's been so brave! I don't want her to worry that I'll abandon her and leave her in animal shape forever."

"Although she seems to have enjoyed her time as a dog," he said with a grin.

"She has," Kirra agreed. "But she'll be human again soon. Let's go buy her a pretty dress at one of the mainland markets so she'll have something special to wear."

They spent hours on Danalustrous, visiting three coastal villages before they found the perfect gift for

Lilah. It was a white cotton frock accented with a bodice of deep red to match her ruby ring. Naturally, they had to find treats for Maria and Cloris and Eileen as well, so they were weighed down with a selection of small packages by the time they made their way back to the island, both of them styled as eagles.

But as they reached the infirmary and circled overhead, they found a knot of people standing outside, clearly waiting for them. Donnal was human before his feet even reached the ground, but it always took Kirra longer to shift. She dropped her burdens and landed lightly, stretching her magnificent wings and tilting her fierce head. A swirl of mist and magic, and she was Kirra again, all gold hair and decisive manner.

"What's wrong?" she demanded. "Did something happen to Lilah?"

Eileen was there with Cloris and one of the other workers, all of them looking dazed and uncertain. Lilah sat at Eileen's feet, panting slightly. Eileen was the one to speak. "We think it's Geena."

Donnal and Kirra exchanged glances. "What does that mean?" Kirra asked.

"Bel's vanished. And Geena's nowhere to be found. But there's a horse standing outside their cabin, looking thin and sick and wasted. Did you change her this morning and forget to tell us?"

Kirra just stared at her. It was Donnal who put the pieces together.

"Bel's a shape-shifter, though she didn't want anyone to know," he said. "She must have changed Geena and then—left."

Now Kirra turned toward him, her face still loose

with disbelief. "A shape-shifter?" she repeated. "Strong enough to transform somebody else?"

"Apparently so. I admit I'm surprised."

"But I thought Geena didn't want to be changed," said Cloris. "She seemed very certain."

"She was," Donnal said grimly. "My guess is that Bel did it without her consent."

"But *why*?"

His eyes were on Kirra, who was still trying to absorb the news that, all this time, there had been another mystic on the island with a power to rival her own. "Because she wanted Geena to live," he said.

"But she was ready to die," Kirra said.

"I know." He gazed at her somberly. "You'll have to change her back."

She started to speak, and he thought the words *Of course!* trembled on her tongue. But then she paused, her eyes locked on his. For a moment, all five of them stood in silence.

"Cloris," Kirra finally said. "Mix up a bowl of the potion, please. The same proportions, but more of it, for a larger animal."

He shook his head. "It won't do any good."

Kirra made the smallest gesture. "I have to try."

He nodded once, sharply, then broke away from the group to charge up the hill. Lilah followed, trotting at his heels.

As soon as he crested the rise, he saw the mare. She was still on her feet, though her legs were braced and her head hung low to the ground as if merely standing was taking all her strength. If she hadn't been so thin, she would have been a handsome animal, graceful and well-formed. The rich caramel color of her coat frayed into festive white spots that dappled her flank, and white stripes added a touch of elegance to her forelegs. Her mane and tail were a rich mahogany, so clean and straight they might have been freshly brushed.

She lifted her head when he moved into view and watched him out of one large brown eye. Even in a face that showed limited emotion, it was easy to read her resignation and sadness. She made no move toward him, but dropped her head when he got close enough and allowed him to rest his cheek against hers. He felt the sleek bristles of her coat prickle against his skin.

"Oh, Geena," he murmured. "What has she done to you?"

He looped an arm around her neck and felt a faint tremble through her heavy body. He doubted that much time would pass before she simply dropped to the grass and refused to get up again. "I suppose she's gone," he said. "This was her final gift or her final betrayal, however you choose to look at it."

Lilah circled the horse once, sniffing the air curiously and barking in an interrogative manner. "Yes, this is Geena," he said, guessing at her question. Lilah barked again, more urgently. "Yes, we could cure her if she wanted to be cured."

Lilah darted forward to nip at the mare's knees, then scooted back before the horse could aim a reflexive kick in her direction. She barked one more time. "You're a fine one to tell people what to do," Donnal scolded. He returned his attention to Geena, running his hand along the wide shoulder.

"You did say you thought it would be glorious to be

an animal," he reminded her. "But this shape will need a little more looking after. I'll bring you some grain and a bucket of water. We carried some apples back from the mainland—you'll like them just as much in this incarnation."

Geena let out a tired, whuffling sound and pulled her head away. He caught her nose in his hand and turned her back.

"No reason you can't keep living, even like this," he said. He stroked the long cheek, brushed his hand down her chest. "You might even find you like it."

At that moment, Kirra strode over the hill a few paces ahead of the others. Lilah dashed over to them, still yapping in excitement, then led them over to where Donnal and Geena waited, as if they wouldn't be able to locate the horse without her help. The islanders hung back; Kirra approached cautiously.

"Hello, Geena," she said. "I wish I'd come by a week or so ago, because I know this seems like a strange way to meet. I'm Kirra Danalustrous."

Even in her altered condition, Geena responded to that name, bobbing her head and turning to give the notorious serramarra a closer inspection. Kirra offered her palm to be sniffed, and Geena nibbled gently at her fingers.

"Obviously, I never met Bel either, but I'm impressed at her ability," Kirra said. "She must be an amazing woman."

Geena closed her eyes and shuffled a few steps backward. Kirra followed, lifting both hands to lay them on either side of the soft mouth. "Speaking as one who has spent some time in this very shape, it's not a bad life," she said. "Sometimes, when I'm in animal form, I find the world much easier to bear. But if you want to be transformed back to your human self, I will do that for you. Today, right now."

She leaned forward, resting her nose against Geena's, her golden hair falling like a mane of its own on either side of Geena's face. "Or you can keep this shape and take the potion," she whispered. "You can live. You choose."

They stood that way for a long moment, motionless, while the others, even Lilah, watched in silence. Then Kirra sighed and stepped back. Cloris crept forward and placed a large clay bowl at Geena's feet. Inside was a generous helping of something that looked like porridge laced with molasses.

Geena tossed her big head, brushed the ground with one hoof, and made a snorting sound. Lilah darted forward again, weaving between Geena's legs, and barking loudly enough to make her own opinion clear. Donnal scooped her up and held her wriggling body close to his.

"You choose," he repeated.

Geena watched him a moment with those huge brown eyes, full of such sorrow and bitter wisdom. Then she lowered her head and began lipping up the concoction, every last bite of it, and licked the empty bowl.

They could not keep Lilah away from Geena. Every time Kirra and Donnal went to check on the newest patient, Lilah was ahead of them. Sometimes the mare and the puppy were idling around the grounds outside the cabin, Geena cropping at the grass, Lilah chasing butterflies or lounging in the sunshine. Twice they were down on the beach, playing in the surf. Lilah raced back and forth with the rushing and receding water, but Geena just paced along, letting the seafoam curl around her hooves and splash up to her knees. She had not entirely lost her air of melancholy, but it was impossible to miss the fact that she was growing stronger. Her heart might still be broken, but her body was starting to mend.

"I hope Geena doesn't mind," Maria said anxiously on the second day. "I think I would have to lock Lilah in her room to stop her from going to her cottage."

"Even if she does mind, it won't be for much longer," Kirra said.

Maria put a hand to her throat. "Tomorrow," she whispered.

The momentous day dawned clear and cool, and it was obvious that none of the main players had been able to sleep much the night before. Donnal and Kirra arrived at the infirmary well before their usual hour to find Cloris, Eileen, Maria, and Lilah already awaiting them in the dining hall.

"I almost can't breathe," Maria choked out.

"Just a few more minutes now," Donnal said.

Kirra bent down and snapped her fingers, and Lilah instantly bounded over. Of all the transformations Kirra had performed, this one was the smoothest and swiftest. One moment, a black-and-brown dog fidgeted on the floor in uncontainable anticipation; the next, a teenage girl stood before her, open-mouthed and wide-eyed.

Maria shrieked and threw her arms around Lilah's nude body. Eileen hurried forward with a blanket and managed to wrap it around Lilah even as the girl jumped up and down with excitement. The next few minutes were happy chaos, as Lilah hugged her mother, hugged Kirra, hugged Donnal, hugged her mother again.

"Are you hungry?" Maria demanded. "What can I get you? Oh, you look so *good!* I can't believe it!"

"Starving. All I can think about is bread!" Lilah replied. "Every day when I ate that gruel, I would think, 'Pretty soon I can have bread again.'"

Cloris turned toward the kitchen. "I've got some fresh-baked right on the counter. And some good butter, too."

Lilah pulled the blanket around herself more tightly and turned toward Donnal, her expression gone serious. "Thank you," she said.

He smiled at her. "Was it as terrifying as you feared?"

"Not once I *did* it. As soon as the—the magic part was done, I wasn't afraid anymore."

He kissed her forehead. "I can't even tell you how happy I am that you agreed."

Now she leaned forward, a look of mischief on her face. "And was it as terrifying as *you* feared?" she whispered, sending a quick glance in Kirra's direction.

"You're a scamp," he informed her, but he couldn't help grinning.

"Was it?"

"Not once I did it." She crowed with laughter and hugged him again.

A few minutes later, they were all sitting around the table, laughing and talking. Joy had sparked their appetites, so they polished off three pots of tea, two loaves of bread, a basket of scones, a jar of honey, and a selection of oranges that Kirra and Donnal had brought back the previous day.

"I think you need a nice bath," Maria said, lifting a lock of Lilah's matted hair. "And then—oh goodness, it will be time to pack up and go! Wait until everyone back home sees you!" She glanced at the others. "Her father will start sobbing. He's such a sweet soul."

"My husband can take you to the mainland tomorrow, if you like," Cloris said.

"We can't go today?"

"All the boats are out on the water already," Eileen explained.

"Oh, of course! Yes, tomorrow would be wonderful."

Lilah was shocked. "We can't leave yet. We have to wait for Geena."

Everyone looked at her in surprise. "Darling," Maria began, but Lilah interrupted.

"I promised I would be here when she was changed back."

Now they all looked at each other, but it was the practical Eileen who voiced their common thought. "I don't see how you could have done that when you weren't even speaking human language."

"Well, I didn't say it in *words*, but she knew that's what I meant."

"Darling," Maria said again.

Kirra was trying not to laugh, but Donnal could see the appreciative amusement in her eyes. Lilah turned to him in appeal.

"Don't you think she wants me here? Don't you

think she needs someone to *support* her? She doesn't *have* anybody else."

"You realize Kirra and I will be here until Kirra changes her back."

Lilah brushed this aside. "That's different. She needs a friend. Someone who understands what it's like."

Donnal smiled at Maria, who was shaking her head. "This one has a good heart," he said. "That's so rare I think you need to give in to it."

Lilah jumped up. "I'm going to tell her right now."

Maria was on her feet just as fast. "No, *first* you're going to take a bath and put on some clothes. I remember what human manners are even if you don't."

"But—"

"The serramarra bought a lovely dress for you to wear on your first day as a girl again. She'll think you're rude if you don't put it on right away. *And* your ruby ring."

"Thank you, serra," Lilah said. "But mama! Let's hurry!"

The two of them were out the door a minute later. Only then did Kirra start laughing, and the sound was so infectious that the rest of them were instantly doubled over in mirth.

"Wild Mother Watch me," Kirra gasped out. "What have I unleashed on the world?"

Eileen had invited Kirra back to her own house so they could, as she put it delicately, discuss some matters that she would like brought to the marlord's attention, if Kirra would be so kind. That was a discussion that obviously excluded Donnal, so for the first time since Geena's transformation, he had a couple of hours alone.

The minute he stepped out of the barracks, he changed to hawk shape and threw himself aloft. Riding the shifting currents, he soared high enough to take in most of the small island with one sweeping glance.

He wasn't sure exactly what he was looking for, but he thought he'd know it when he saw it. A stony outcropping atop an inhospitable climb, a place difficult enough to attain that few people would bother to go there. Close enough to the infirmary that a short flight would bring it into view but far enough away that no one would often think to glance in that direction.

He circled in an ever-tightening pattern until he found a likely spot, a narrow ledge of rock against a mound of boulders that formed a bulwark against the incessant wind. In the center was a single squat tree that looked as if it had clawed its way up the mountain and stayed, too stubborn to retreat or die. There was another hawk already perched in the spiky branches, its feathers ruffling against the gusting air.

Donnal dropped lower, slowly enough to catch the attention of the other creature, who watched his approach with fierce yellow eyes. He curled his talons around a convenient branch, steadied himself, and folded his wings.

They regarded each other for a moment. The other hawk was larger, more powerful, no doubt female. She bridled then resettled, still staring. Donnal merely waited. With a toss of her head, she spread her wings, hopped from the tree and glided to the ground. Her transformation from avian to human shape was fluid and elegant, like a spin of leaves in an autumn storm, and suddenly Bel stood before him.

He dropped to the ground and made his own swift conversion. She watched in silence and waited for him to speak.

"It's never quite as easy to leave as you expect, is it?" he asked.

She shrugged. "I wanted to wait long enough to see what she would choose. And it seems she has decided to live."

"Not that you care."

"I do care. Just not enough to stay."

"How long do you plan to stick around? Until she's human again? Will you follow her to the mainland so you can check up on her from time to time—always in animal form, of course, never showing her your true self? So *you* have the satisfaction of knowing how she fares, while *she* is left to wonder about you for the rest of her life?"

"Well, you already accused me of being selfish. I suppose you can't be surprised."

"How long did you skulk around nearby," he asked, "after Kirra was born?"

Now she was silent even longer, her eyes locked on his face. He wasn't sure she would answer—and why should she? He half-expected her to slip back into bird shape to flee his uncomfortable questions. But when she began shifting, she kept her basic human form, merely altering some of her curves and hollows. Now her cheekbones were sharp, her hair a ripple of curls, her eyes a careless blue. Yes, he would have recognized her. She had been right to adopt a disguise.

She held his gaze a long moment, then shrugged again and looked away. "I stayed for two years after she was born—stayed all that time styled as a human, nursing her and tending her like a doting mother. But I was so restless I wanted to scratch my skin open just to let my blood run wild, even if I couldn't. One night I gave her to the maid and stepped outside of Danan Hall and turned myself into the daintiest little songbird you ever saw. And I flew away."

She glanced back at him, then returned her attention to the view. "Oh, you're right. I remained nearby for a few months, watching through the windows. There were some nights she cried—I could hear the sound even through the glass. But someone was always at her side within a minute. The nurse or the maid or even Malcolm himself, holding her in his arms and rocking her to sleep. *Malcolm*, who could never be bothered to care for anybody until Kirra came along."

She reached up absently to snap a small branch from the skeletal tree and began systematically stripping off the leaves. "And then I left for a week. And came back for three days. And left for a month. And came back for two days. As the years went by, I returned less and less often, but I already knew what I needed to know. She was cared-for and content. She had no need of me."

"And if that hadn't been the case? If she had been lonely and desperate, ignored by her father and mistreated by her stepmother? Would you have stepped in to save her?"

Her gaze on his face was remote and cool. "I don't know," she said. "The question didn't arise."

"How many other children have you left behind

because it was too much trouble to take them with you?"

She surprised him by laughing. "None," she said. "Do you think a shape-shifter can't control her body? I knew better than to allow myself to get pregnant a second time. I only agreed to have Kirra to satisfy Malcolm."

"And how soon do you think it was before he wasn't quite so satisfied?"

"You think he was shocked to learn he married a mystic? He married me *because* I was a mystic." She laughed again at his thunderstruck expression. "He looked around and saw magic beginning to seep through Gillengaria, growing stronger and more powerful after centuries of lying dormant. He thought, 'How can I turn that into an advantage for Danalustrous?' He *wanted* a child with sorcery in her veins."

Donnal was still too stunned to ask more questions, but Bel went on unprompted, her voice almost pensive with memory.

"He came wooing me at my brother's estate, offering me any bargain I would like. I went by the name Balyn then. 'Tell me what you want, Balyn,' he said every day. 'And I'll give it to you.' I knew even then I couldn't possibly become some dull, docile marlady, listening to the petitions of aggrieved farmers and presiding over tedious balls. I said, 'All I want is my freedom.' And he said, 'Give me one daughter, and you can be free of me forever.'"

She shrugged again. "Malcolm Danalustrous is a hard man to resist. And I thought it would be interesting, for at least a little while, to be rich and pampered and powerful. And it was." She turned a hand palm-up. "And then it wasn't."

He drew a slow, deep breath. It was almost impossible to know how to respond. How could two such supremely arrogant people have created the magnificence that was Kirra? Hardly any wonder that she could be haughty, thoughtless, and rash—it was more astonishing that she could be loyal and tender and true. Was that her stepmother's gentling influence? Her sister's? Even Senneth's? Or was it just her own great heart, haphazardly constructed but generous and faithful and full of joy? He didn't think there had ever been a moment he had loved her more.

"Thank you for explaining it to me," he said, and let her judge if he was being sincere or ironic.

She studied him a moment. "Are you going to tell her about me?"

He returned her regard steadily. "Why would I? How could it possibly make her life better to know you're still alive?"

Her expression flared with hostility. "I just thought. If she was curious. You've learned some of the answers."

Now he was the one to shrug. "I don't believe she thinks about you any more than you think about her."

This time she didn't let herself react. "And will you tell Geena that I'm still here watching over her?"

"I think if you want people to forgive you for leaving, you'll have to make your own goodbyes."

"How pleasant it must be for you," she snapped, "to have no flaws of your own."

"Many flaws," he said. "But I know how to love somebody."

He didn't bother with more conversation. He lifted his arms, tucked in his elbows, transformed into the shape of a crow, and took off. The relentless wind off the ocean buffeted him about, causing him to tack and bob, but he traveled steadily toward the small cabin on the center of the island, and never for a minute did he lose his way.

CHAPTER 14

Five of them gathered to witness Kirra return Geena to her human form. Cloris had made a cake and Eileen had brought a lovely linen dress that she'd made "because it's like a rebirth, isn't it, and she should have a new outfit for the occasion." Lilah was there because no power in the world would have kept her away, and Maria was there to keep Lilah in check.

Donnal draped a wool blanket over the mare's dappled coat, which had grown shiny and luxuriant as she returned to health. "We don't want even such a shabby noble as you to be naked and embarrassed in front of us," he said, stroking her broad nose. She gave a very unladylike snort and nibbled at his ear.

"If we're all ready," Kirra said, and Geena bowed her head into Kirra's outstretched hands. Donnal could tell by Kirra's intent expression that it took a significant amount of energy to transform such a huge creature back to its natural state, and he wondered if the fact that she was reversing someone else's magic made the feat even harder. But before he had time to feel more than a shiver of fear, the horse began to shimmer and shrink and reconfigure itself.

And then suddenly a woman was kneeling on the ground, half-resting on the heels of her hands, swathed in the blanket and gazing around with bemused, blinking eyes.

"Geena!" Lilah cried and flung her arms around the woman's neck. "You look wonderful!"

In the instant before she answered, Geena turned to give Donnal one quick glance of acknowledgment. In her green eyes, he saw pain and resignation and something that might be brighter—hope, he thought, or at least the belief that healing might be possible sometime in the future. Then she smiled and wrapped her wool-clad arms around the young girl.

"Hello, Lilah. I am so happy to finally meet you face to face."

They all adjourned to the dining hall for a celebratory feast. Lilah plunked herself down right next to Geena and chattered away unselfconsciously while the rest of them ate. Geena seemed abstracted, as if still trying to accustom herself to the tighter confines of her human body.

Or maybe something else kept tugging at her attention. More than once, Donnal caught her watching Kirra with a sidelong, helpless fascination. He had wondered how much she knew of Bel's past and her connection with Malcolm Danalustrous, and by her expression, he was pretty sure he had the answer. He would never ask her outright; he would never tell anyone of his final conversation with Balyn. And he was fairly certain this was knowledge that Geena would keep to herself forever. Her last gift to Bel, perhaps, or her first act of gratitude to Kirra.

Despite the high spirits of their little group, the mood was wistful. The hall seemed overlarge and empty, full of ghosts and memories, and a heavy sense of finality underlay all their light words.

"Of course, I'm *happy* that everyone is well now, but it seems very strange that everyone is gone," Cloris said with a sigh. "I miss caring for so many people."

"We'll have to think of something else to do with the place," Eileen said. "Must be some kind of use for a nice big building like this."

"You don't think you'll be getting more patients with red-horse fever?" Maria asked.

"Doesn't seem like it. We haven't had any new ones for a few weeks now. Maybe the disease has burned itself out."

"And good riddance," Cloris added.

"Turn it into a hotel," Kirra suggested. "For the world-weary nobles who want to pretend they'd like to live the simple life." She glanced around. "Although you might need to install more amenities."

"Make it an orphanage," Geena said. "A school. There must be plenty of children on the mainland who could use a safe place to live."

Eileen looked intrigued. "That's an interesting thought," she said. "I wonder if Malcolm Danalustrous could be counted on to fund it."

Kirra laughed. "Well, no one can *ever* speak for my father, but I would think he would be happy to. I'll ask him when I see him in Ghosenhall—which should be very soon. I'm overdue as it is."

"Will you leave tonight?" Eileen asked.

"Tomorrow," Donnal answered before Kirra could reply. "She doesn't think she's tired, but today's magic took a toll on her, and she needs to rest."

Kirra scowled at him. "I'll be glad when you stop fussing about me so much."

"I think it's nice to be fussed over from time to time," Eileen said.

Cloris glanced mournfully between Maria, Lilah, and Geena. "I suppose the three of you will be sailing off tomorrow with the morning tide."

"On the first boat that will take us," Maria agreed. "My husband could barely restrain himself from coming to Dorrin Isle when I wrote to tell him about the cure. But of course, someone had to stay with the farm."

Geena wore a pensive expression. "I might stay a little longer," she said. Donnal could tell that she was trying to keep her voice casual. "There's no place I'm in a particular hurry to get back to." She gestured at the high ceiling. "Maybe I'll stay here and teach in the new school."

Lilah hastily swallowed a mouthful of food. "You can come live with us," she offered.

"*Lilah!*" Maria exclaimed, regarding her with horror. "You can't—nobles don't just come live with farmers."

"She could have my room," Lilah said. "I'll sleep in the barn. I spend the night there in the summer half the time," she explained to the table. "Especially once the baby calves start coming."

Maria addressed Geena awkwardly. "Forgive her— she doesn't understand—she thinks it's a kindness—"

Geena touched her slim fingers to Maria's work-roughened hand. "It *is* a kindness," she said. "I would never presume to present myself at your homestead, but if there's a town nearby and a respectable inn—" She laughed suddenly, which momentarily chased away the sadness etched into her face. "Or even not so respectable. I've stayed in plenty of questionable lodgings during my last few years of travel."

"Good, then that's settled," Lilah said. "Cloris, did you say there was pie?"

Donnal could tell by Maria's expression that she didn't think it was settled, but he had the feeling that Lilah and Geena would conspire to make the visit happen. He couldn't think it would be a long-term solution to the question that would vex Geena in the coming weeks: What exactly would she do with this life that she had been given, despite the fact she hadn't wanted it? She might mend relations with her family, he thought. She might return to Dorrin Isle. She might find herself addicted enough to the pleasures of travel that she continued to journey from town to town, seeking occasional adventures and perhaps making new friends. He would guess she had enough money to fund an itinerant lifestyle, especially since she didn't seem to care much for fancy clothes and grand accommodations.

He smiled at her across the table. "It might take a while, but you'll find your way," he said.

"Not the one I was expecting," she said wryly.

He nodded. "It so rarely is."

The rest of the day was both bittersweet and unsettled. The five travelers were impatient to be gone, yet somewhat despondent at the thought that they would be leaving behind a place where they had experienced such monumental events and forged such powerful bonds.

"It seems strange to think that I'll never see any of them again," Kirra said to Donnal that night as they lay on the pallet before the dying fire. "Companions of the road! I've made many along the way. But it seems different this time."

He smoothed back the golden curls that had tumbled free during their lovemaking. "You can watch them sail away tomorrow and just suppose that they will lead interesting lives with the usual measure of joy and regret," he said. "Or you could check in now and then from a distance. Fly over Maria's farm and see how tall Lilah's grown. Turn yourself into a cat and prowl through whatever inn or manor Geena has decided to call home."

The firelight played across her face, which was drawn into a slight frown. "I don't like that idea."

He smiled and kissed her forehead. "Or you can go visit them, styled as Kirra Danalustrous," he said. "Bring them presents. Stay for tea. They'll be delighted to see you. They'll welcome you into their lives."

"That's what I'll do," she said drowsily, resting her forehead against his chest. "In a few months, maybe. Or once a year. That sounds good, doesn't it?"

He kissed her again. "It sounds perfect."

They both slept uneasily and woke before dawn.

"Time to go," Kirra whispered, and he nodded.

They stepped outside into the cool, fresh air, turning their eyes toward the eastern horizon. A glimmer of gold outlined the low peaks of Dorrin Isle and hinted at the great mass of Gillengaria just beyond. Donnal felt his blood stir with the old restlessness, the neverending desire to be in motion.

"To Ghosenhall?" he asked.

"If you'll come with me."

"Anywhere."

She kissed him, and then she changed. She was a woman, she was a shadow, she was a small brown bird, a swift, built for days of uninterrupted travel. Donnal swirled into a companion shape and together they lifted themselves into the inviting air. The world below them was just waking up, and the terrain before them beckoned with its own unimaginable wonders. Impossible to know where this new journey would take them. They rode and coasted on the playful winds, headed toward land, toward adventure, toward whatever the next day would bring.

ABOUT THE AUTHOR

Sharon Shinn has published 33 novels, three short fiction collections, and one graphic novel since she joined the science fiction and fantasy world in 1995. She has written about angels, shape-shifters, elemental powers, magical portals, and echoes. She has won the William C. Crawford Award for Outstanding New Fantasy Writer, a Reviewer's Choice Award from the Romantic Times, and the 2010 RT Book Reviews Career Achievement Award in the Science Fiction/Fantasy category. Follow her at SharonShinnBooks on Facebook or visit her website. Try sharonshinn.net first, but if that doesn't work, she has relocated to sharonshinn.info

OTHER TITLES FROM FAIRWOOD PRESS

*Obviously I Love You
But If I Were a Bird*
by Patrick O'Leary
small paperback $11.00
ISBN: 978-1-958880-37-1

Space Trucker Jess
by Matthew Kressel
trade paper $20.95
ISBN: 978-1-958880-27-2

One Last Game
by T.A. Chan
trade paper $15.99
ISBN: 978-1-958880-34-0

When Mothers Dream: Stories
by Brenda Cooper
trade paper $18.99
ISBN: 978-1-958880-35-7

*Better Dreams, Fallen Seeds
and Other Handfuls of Hope*
by Ken Scholes
paperback $19.99
ISBN: 978-1-958880-32-6

Changelog: Collected Fiction
by Rich Larson
trade paper $20.95
ISBN: 978-1-958880-33-3

Black Hole Heart and Other Stories
by K.A. Teryna
trade paper $18.99
ISBN: 978-1-958880-29-6

*A Catalog of Storms:
Collected Short Fiction*
by Fran Wilde
trade paper $18.99
ISBN: 978-1-958880-31-9

Find us at:
www.fairwoodpress.com
Bonney Lake, Washington